I0771467

In My Opinion

My Journey To Spiritual Well Being

Ed Cubilla

Copyright © 2024

LCCN: 2024926083
eBook ISBN: 978-1-966373-72-8
Paperback ISBN: 978-1-966373-70-4
Hardcover ISBN: 978-1-966373-71-1

All Rights Reserved. Any unauthorized reprint or use of this material is strictly prohibited. No part of this book may be reproduced or transmitted in any form or by any means, electronic or mechanical, including photocopying, recording, or by any information storage and retrieval system without express written permission from the author.

All reasonable attempts have been made to verify the accuracy of the information provided in this publication. Nevertheless, the author assumes no responsibility for any errors and/or omissions.

Disclaimer: This non-fiction work is rooted in the author's personal experiences and true events. The names mentioned in this book exclusively pertain to individuals who played a role in the author's journey and are included for the sake of narrative clarity. It is important to note that the use of names is not intended to offend or target any specific individual. The author respects the privacy and dignity of all those involved and has taken care to present the events accurately and responsibly.

I like to thank Penguin Book Writers for their efforts in editing this material to acceptable publication standards.

Dedicated to my three sons: Omar, David, and Elvio, and my seven granddaughters, Genevieve, Emily, Tiani, Georgia, Sienna, Eva, and Remi.

Contents

Preface

I titled this work "In My Opinion" as a sign of respect to my brother in the faith, mentor, and friend Martin. He argued that I was too dogmatic in regard to how I believe in the Bible and the Bible alone, and he often said that I should be more flexible regarding religious doctrines created by men. I explained to him that I did not have opinions and that I only quoted passages of the Bible and, if at all, I had 'educated opinions.' This is my modest effort to elaborate on those 'educated opinions.'

Part 1

Chapter One – My Non-Religious Background

"El Blanquito," moving through the evening traffic, made its way down the busy Mitre Avenue. The sounds of loud horns, car engines working hard, and people talking about football and politics mixed together. It was like a song that you would only hear at night in Buenos Aires.

In the city, bus drivers did a great job every day. They drove in the morning, afternoon, and night, taking lots of people where they needed to go. The roads were always packed, so they had to be very careful when they drove.

My family liked to use this bus company. The buses were named Blanquitos because they were white. Blanquito means "the little white one," a friendly way to talk about them. They had route number 120, and they were special because they were the only buses owned by the state until they were sold to private owners. My uncle Juan worked for this company. He was a conductor and really proud of his job. These tickets were cheaper than others, which was why we liked them.

I remember when I was a little boy, one trip with my mom when we were coming back from the hospital. It was just a normal day on the bus. Some people were sleeping, some were thinking, and some were just sitting there. Everyone looked tired like they just wanted to get home.

But then, something interesting happened. Almost at the same time, everyone started making a gesture with their right hand, touching their faces and chests, and then they stopped and went back to how they were before.

When this happened, my mom would take my hand, and we would get ready to get off. We would press the bell and wait for the bus to stop. That was where we needed to get off.

During a lot of my time in high school, I got used to watching people on the bus make a certain hand gesture to know when my stop was coming up. But as I got older, not as many people made this gesture, so it wasn't as helpful for knowing when to get off. That meant I had to start looking for other things outside the bus to tell me when my stop was near.

This hand gesture that people did on the bus was actually a special religious thing. It's called the sign of the cross, and it's something Catholic people do. I didn't know what it meant for a while. Later, I figured out that people did it as a way to show respect when we drove past a certain church, the Parroquia Nuestra Señora de Loreto, on Mitre Avenue in Avellaneda was one of them.

A few years after I first noticed this on the bus, I saw the same gesture again, but this time at a football match. It must have been a big game because there were more people in the streets and the stadium than I had ever seen before. The game was at the Racing Club stadium in Avellaneda. The whole place felt like a big party. There was loud music playing from speakers, and blue and white streamers were hung all around. The air smelled of peanuts being roasted nearby. Fans from both teams were there, cheering and singing loudly for their teams. Now and then, cars and buses honked their horns, adding to the noise and fun.

The fans were really into the game, trying to outdo each other by being loud and excited. They shouted, jumped around, and banged on big drums painted in the colors of their teams. All this noise and excitement made the whole afternoon feel alive. It was such an amazing thing to see and be a part of.

That afternoon was a special one for me. Racing Club got a penalty kick, and if they scored, it would tie the game since it was almost the end of the match. The best part for me was when Toti, my cousin, lifted me onto his shoulders. This let me see the game much better. I always saw other kids being lifted up like this at games, but it was my first time experiencing it.

Toti was the one who introduced me to Racing Club when I was nine. In Argentina, it's pretty late to start supporting a football team. Usually, even little kids wear jerseys of their parents' favorite teams. I didn't have a dad around; he left us when I was seven. So Toti was the one who got me into Racing Club and brought me to the games.

From Toti's shoulders, I could see the penalty kick clearly. But what caught my eye was how both the goalkeeper from the other team and the Racing player taking the kick made the same hand gesture before the kick. Racing scored, tying, or maybe even winning the game.

After that, I started noticing that hand gesture more often. It seemed like it was always there, but I hadn't paid attention before. It was interesting because I used to see it a lot on the bus, and now I was seeing it in completely different places.

Another time, Julio, who was going to be my stepdad, took me to Luna Park to see a wrestling show, "Titanes en el Ring." I had watched it on TV, but seeing it live was a different experience. The wrestlers would do the same gesture when they came out to the ring and before the match started. I wasn't sure what to make of it. It was surprising because it didn't seem like a respectful gesture in the middle of all the rough fighting. Maybe they were asking for protection from getting hurt, or maybe they were hoping to beat their opponent badly. I guess I'll never really know. Boxers also practiced this gesture. Right before their fights, each boxer, standing in their corner of the ring, would kneel on one knee and cross themselves. This action, I believe, wasn't really about showing respect. It seemed more like they were asking for the strength to defeat their opponent, perhaps even hoping to land a knockout blow.

This gesture, similar to the one I saw on the bus and at the football match, took on a different meaning in my eyes. It became less about respect and more like a good luck charm. For example, one of my friends always carried a lucky sock, kissing it for good luck before our soccer games. With no religious upbringing, how else could I have understood these gestures? They seemed like just another form of wishing for good luck.

It's important to mention that I was aware of the belief in God, but I never truly grasped its meaning. Some books argue that belief in God is due to early indoctrination. However, in my case, and I suspect in many others, this wasn't true. I've often heard people say they felt religion was forced upon them, and as they grew older, they moved away from it, identifying as atheists, agnostics, or other non-religious labels.

Growing up in an atheist and materialistic household, the concept of God and religious practices were often looked upon with skepticism. We leaned more toward science, evidence, and the theory of evolution. By the age of eleven, I became acquainted with various social and political concepts – not because they were household topics, but because I found and read materials lying around at home. These ideas, such as the exploitation of the working class, class struggle, and the concept of surplus value, intrigued me, even though they were not common topics of discussion among my family. More often, the talk at home revolved around practical matters like government policies or the rising cost of living.

My favorite saying was 'we seek the elimination of the exploitation of men by men." If I have to use it today, I would say, "We seek the elimination of the exploitation of nature and men by men."

Our home was different from the usual 'nuclear family' setup. My mother was the backbone, tirelessly working to support her two children. She juggled her job washing and ironing clothes for others with her night classes at nursing school, run by the Red Cross. Her determination paid off when she got a job as a nurse at a local clinic, yet she continued doing laundry work even while working full-time at the clinic. She was an incredible woman, always busy, often bent over the washboard, tirelessly scrubbing clothes while whistling a tune.

My sister was in school, too, and as she grew up, she began tutoring high school students to earn some extra money. This meant she was rarely at home as well. For a long time, it was just the three of us doing what we could to get by.

We faced tough times, with poverty hitting us hard. My mom had two jobs, and my sister balanced her studies with tutoring work. Despite these challenges, I never saw them turn to religious rituals for comfort. They never did the sign of the cross or sought blessings in that way. Perhaps, in hindsight, it might have brought them some solace.

Chapter Two – My Early Ideology And The Son of Man

One day, after school, I came home to find the doors locked, and nobody was there. I had to climb over a wooden wall to get inside our apartment. Inside, I found myself in a small hallway with just a table and a couple of chairs, as the bedrooms were all locked. Sitting there, alone and hungry, I didn't know what to do. I looked around and saw an interesting piece of furniture. It was a bookcase with two glass doors, but you couldn't see the books because of a dirty, brownish curtain that was a bit torn. I got closer and could smell the musty scent of old paper. The bookcase was full of old books, and it belonged to my father.

I was never much into reading or doing homework, but for some reason, I felt like picking up one of those books. I think the first book I chose was "The Complete Works of Lenin." There was a phrase in there that stuck with me. It went something like, "If there's a half apple, there must be another half somewhere else." That really made me think and seemed deep to me. So, I started reading all the books I could find in that bookcase. This became my routine: coming home, feeling hungry, and reading. I wasn't a fast reader and still am not, so it took me a while to get through each book.

I read a mix of stories, like "The Champion," "Ivanhoe," "The Quixote of the Mancha," "White Fang," "Robinson Crusoe," "How the Steel was Tempered," "The Little Prince," and "Humpy Dumpy." There were probably others, but I don't remember them all. I also read non-fiction books about Lenin, Marx, Engels, and the history of Argentina. Honestly, I don't think I understood much of what I read, whether it was fiction or not.

I did absorb a few basic ideas:

Ruling class: those who own the means of production and capital (probably one and the same).

Struggle of classes: even today, I am not sure what that means. Probably something like they have the money and power, and we don't.

'Surplus value.' At the time the worker gets paid wages, there is exploitation as the worker does not get the total value of the labor performed. I took that as being the profit component.

'Religion.' The opium of the people. Used to keep workers exploited and in a state of submission.

"Reactionary." The system kills workers who want equality, higher wages, and better working conditions.

My social conscience has been guided by these ideas, rightfully or wrongly. The one thing I can claim, though, is that there were no religious ideas of any type. That is not completely true. Before my father abandoned us before my seventh birthday, I remember he told me a religious joke.

There was a story about a man who loved to gamble. He was down to his last bit of money and decided to bet it all on a horse named "Fleas," which was racing that coming weekend. He went to a nearby church and, standing in front of a statue of Saint Peter, made a bold promise. He asked the statue to ensure Fleas won the race, and if not, he threatened to come back and smash the statue with a hammer. A priest nearby overheard this and got really worried. He told another priest, and they decided to move the big statue and put a small, cheap one in its place.

Well, Fleas didn't win the race. So, the gambler came back, hammer in hand, ready to keep his word. When he saw the small statue, he joked, "Little Peter, where's your father?" That joke was the closest thing to a religious talk in our home.

Our life was a lot like the bus El Blanquito, navigating through life's ups and downs. We'd sometimes stop, then move forward, seizing opportunities when we could. Not taking those chances could mean getting stuck longer than necessary. Sometimes, we'd have to backtrack a bit to find a better path. Life required careful maneuvers, a mix of boldness and caution, conviction and hesitation. Everything had its place in our journey, filled with many twists and turns.

One of the most impactful moments for me came when I was thinking about becoming an actor. At eighteen, I got to meet a legend in the Argentinian world of theatre, radio, and film – Mr. Guillermo Battaglia. He was a real star, known for his extensive career across different platforms. Meeting him was a significant event that sparked my curiosity and interest in the world of acting.

I answered a newspaper ad about acting classes, and at my first class, I couldn't believe who I saw. It was someone I had recognized from movies, and I was completely starstruck.

He wasn't exactly humble, but he was more than willing to share his knowledge. He taught me the basics of acting – how to breathe properly and how to use my voice effectively. He suggested I read Stanislavski's works and showed me how to apply those teachings. My favorite part was characterization: reading and acting out scripts. But then, life took a turn. Mr. Battaglia moved away from Buenos Aires to live in the countryside, and that was the end of my lessons with him.

A year later, I auditioned for a theater play and got a part. The director, who was also our acting coach, was the most intriguing person I've ever met. He often talked about being a Gnostic. He would explain how the seven churches in the Book of Revelation related to the seven chakras along the human spine and how opening these chakras through meditation could lead to enlightenment.

He had some pretty forward-thinking ideas, especially for Argentina around 1971. He talked about the Age of Aquarius, a time when God separated men and women. He believed that in the future, gay love would become common and accepted, which was a bold statement for that time. He even said that the acceptance of homosexuality was a necessary step towards men and women becoming one gender again. His ideas were definitely out there!

He also talked about Genesis marking the start of the Age of Aquarius, when the genders were separated. But what really caught my attention was when he talked about the "Son of Man." Every time he mentioned this character, his face lit up with fascination. He made this "Son of Man" seem like the most extraordinary person to ever walk the earth.

Even though Mr. De La Plaza's talks were intriguing, I didn't really know what to make of them. But they did make me curious. Who was this Son of Man? How could I learn more about him? Terms like Genesis, Apocalypse, and Son of Man didn't mean much to me back then. Why would they?

However, my time in the acting world was brief. The need to earn a living and focus on high school brought me back to reality. Dreams of acting took a back seat to more practical concerns. And with that, the "Son of Man" faded from my immediate thoughts, but the curiosity he sparked never completely left my mind.

Chapter Three – Australia & The Son of Man

The twists and turns of life brought me to Australia in 1974. As far as adventures went, this one was the most significant of my young life.

My friend Eduardo was of Yugoslavian descent. He told me that he believed his father was Yugoslavian and that there were a few Yugoslavians in his neighborhood. Eduardo used to tell me that his father and compatriots used to meet at the street corner near his house and, under the street lamp at night, talked about Tito. Apparently, my friend was not too keen about these people talking in a foreign language, and he said the only thing he understood was "Tito." Also, he assumed they were not all Yugoslavian but from that region. Of course, it is common knowledge that Argentina had a large influx of Europeans migrating there in search of a new life after the Second World War. My friend's father was one of them.

While Don Juan migrated to Argentina, his brother (Eduardo's uncle) migrated to Melbourne, Australia. One time, while Eduardo and I were still completing our Diploma in Engineering, his uncle visited Argentina. All I remember is that these brothers resembled each other, and I never forgot what the uncle said to us in broken Spanish/Italian: "When you finish your studies, go to Australia. Molto moneta," and rubbed his thumb and index finger. Clear enough for us.

My friend took the idea of going to Australia very seriously, and he told me he would go if I went too. He would not go alone. I said that I would, and I did.

Part of my preparations to come to Australia was getting married to my girlfriend. The idea was for me to see what it was like in Australia. If it passed my assessment, she would join me. The preparations for my friend were to practice driving on the wrong side of the road, learn English, and save money.

The initial cultural shock of being 16000 km away from home and waking up in a former army cabin disappeared when I stepped out of the cabin and experienced the most beautiful 9th of August morning of my life.

My cabin, C42, was part of a former army barracks at Wacol, a suburb in Brisbane, Australia. By the time I arrived in Australia in 1974, this army barrack was transformed into a migrant hostel. And it was here where these glorious mornings witnessed the beginning of a new way of life for me.

We arrived in Brisbane on a Thursday; the following Monday, we were already working. We were part of a construction gang; my job was to dig pipeline holes in an open camp using a jackhammer. These holes were to be used to lay down water pipes for the development of a brand-new suburb called Bellbowrie.

These beautiful mornings saw me challenging myself to get another job, this one in a slaughterhouse at J.C Huttons – Small Goods, Oxley Road, Oxley. From jackhammer to working in the cold room, packing ham in plastic net bags, and pushing carcasses deep into the refrigerated rooms. I loved this job; I made friends, one of whom is still my friend, as I wrote these words forty-something years later. I made good money; I worked hard for short hours.

Once a quota was completed, and the last carcass put away, we cleaned our working area, and off we were - sometimes as early as midday, having started at 7.30 am and a brief 'smoko.' From there, I would go to the Corinda municipal swimming pool and usually meet some of my friends from the hostel there. I could not swim, but just being in a swimming pool was the greatest feeling as I had never been in a swimming pool before in my life. My friend Eduardo went to Melbourne; I stayed back in Brisbane.

I was working, saving money, and enjoying the company of new friends from all around the world. Particularly, I enjoyed the company of Chilean refugees who had escaped the dictatorship of Pinochet in 1973. I was surprised to find out that the status of refugees was granted to them in Peru for the majority of them, and they carried with them an official stamp of the United Nations on their passports.

So, sunny, warm, clear blue winter skies, walking around in shirt sleeves, plenty of new friends, money – was this paradise or what?

To complete this new idyllic life, I was able to buy a car in only a few weeks of being in Australia. It was a second-hand 1968 Holden Kingswood. Not my first car, mind you; I bought a Fiat 600 with my friend Eduardo in Argentina. We shared ownership, and it worked quite well until I crashed it. I was not going to crash this one, though.

I was not the first one in the Migrant Hostel to buy a car. From the people I knew, a friend from South America bought a small white two-door Torana practically the same week we touched soil in Brisbane. He was one of the very few who could speak English fluently. Both he and his wife had visited and spent some time in the USA. They were dancers specializing in typical South American folklore. Although we don't keep in touch as much as we would like, I still consider them some of the most influential people in my life.

I am not sure how, but somehow, we discussed Gnosticism. The topic probably came about talking about theatre, performing, and acting, and I mentioned my theatre teacher and director, R. de la Plaza, who was a Gnostic.

As it happened, this young couple were practicing Gnostics themselves, and when I showed an interest in the matter, they were kind enough to lend me one of their books. The title of the book escapes me now, but there were references there to "The Son of Man." After many years of this character having made an appearance in my life, there it was again.

It was through this Gnostic book that I learned the connection between the Son of Man and the Bible. The author used the names Jesus and Son of Man interchangeably, referring to the same person. I remember clearly the book made the claim that Jesus walked on water in the state of "Jinas." Apparently, this mystic state is achieved through meditation; the person leaves the body and travels in some form of astral manifestation. The book explained that was the reason the disciples saw Jesus sleeping on the beach and his ghost walking on water towards them. The book also went on to other fascinating aspects of this character. Through harnessing mental powers, this character could become invisible, change appearance, and heal people, among other gifts.

Who wouldn't want to know more about him?

It was in the middle of this state of affairs that something really remarkable happened to me.

Life in a migrant hostel is richer than it is possible to imagine from the outside. I will not go into the details of the mixing of beautiful people from all over the world in a relatively closed (and close) environment. But I will remark a very interesting feature of it.

One of the various places for social meetings in the hostel was the front yard of the post office; it was really a car park. The PO met some basic characteristics that made it an attractive meeting point. We could post our mail there, obviously pick up our mail, and more importantly, it had a couple of phones from which overseas calls were possible. Interestingly enough, these international calls were not possible from all public phones at the time. Even at the

Central Post Office in Queen Street, Brisbane, phones were specially allocated for that business.

One morning, out of nowhere, I headed straight to the PO at the hostel. There, in what I now think was a desperate and impulsive act, I asked a group of about twenty Marxist refugees if someone had a Bible. I explained that I wanted to know about the Son of Man and that I believed I could find some references about him in the Bible.

After a brief silence that seemed to go on for hours, they shook their heads in an emphatic no. I still remember the looks on their faces. Confused, disconcerted, but mostly in total disbelief that somebody would have the nerve to ask them such a question. Most of them looked at the ground, then each other, and then they focused on me, probably to see if I meant it or if I was joking.

I went back to my cabin to read the Gnostic book; I fell asleep for a while when I heard a knock on the door. I did not realize it, but it was just after midday. I must have slept for a while.

I opened the door and saw El Chico Roberto.

There was something about El Chico Roberto; he was short but solid. His small, dark eyes seemed to be toying with you all the time. He emanated the type of self-assurance that people would easily interpret as 'this guy is not one to be messed around with.' Yet, he was always respectful and kind.

"You said you wanted a Bible?"

"Yes, I think the Son of Man is mentioned there."

"Well, I don't have a Bible, but I have this, which is part of the Bible. This kept me safe everywhere I went; it brought me safely here."

"Are you sure you want to give it to me?"

"Yes, I am sure."

I saw it was a little book, so I said, "Okay, when I finish with it, I will give it back to you."

"No, it's okay for you to keep it." I thanked him. In my mind, I was going to return his little book as soon as I finished reading it. I calculated it would not take me long, being such a small book. I could tell the little book had its fair share of use. The dark blue cover was worn out, its original color fading in some places, and the spine edges displayed the white undercover binding paper.

We said our goodbyes, and he left. I perused the book very quickly; the lettering was small but readable, the pages yellowish, and the whole structure surprisingly sturdy. That little book could take a beating, and my guess was that it had.

I laid down on my bed and started reading. My eyes were rushing down the sentences, and I was turning pages extremely fast. I was not actually reading; I was scanning for the mysterious phrase "Son of Man." The first instance I noticed the phrase, it was actually Jesus talking about "The Son of Man." I wanted to read more. I wanted to see why my theatre director/tutor spoke so highly of the Son of Man.

So the adventure began, as they say.

From the time I took possession of the New Testament, as the book was titled, it was part of my daily routine to read it, enjoy it, and savor it. I don't think I could provide even an educated guess as to how many times I have read it.

My interest was mainly in the Gospels, to digest it, to take it apart almost automatically. I did not have a schedule or anything methodically in place, but I have read the Gospels many times. Made connections about the Son of Man and practically everything else mentioned in those pages. I tried to read the rest of the book, the epistles, the Book of Revelation, and the Psalms, but none of them really kept my interest, and invariably I came back to the Gospels.

My favorite book was the Gospel of Matthew; it is still my favorite. I completely love this Gospel. I mostly focused on what Jesus said. How He treated people, what He taught, how He taught, and I liked it. I enjoyed it when He dished it out to the rich, greedy people, and I liked it even more when He served it to the religious people. I thought Jesus was less religious than me.

Of course, I was completely taken by His person, but the actual theology of it all was lost on me. I did not know what He was actually doing and, most importantly, what He did.

Eventually, I ventured onto the other books of the New Testament. They did not tell me much, and I did not enjoy reading them because I could not see what they were trying to tell or teach. I know now that was because the epistles are mainly instructions to believers. Which, at that stage, I wasn't.

I said I wasn't a believer because I wasn't in the conventional sense. To me, Jesus was a real historical person trying to teach very powerful concepts to His people. In my mind, He took on the religious system and the people who control power through the religious system. Those powerful people didn't like that and made Him pay the price. To me, Jesus was a real character of the time. In the same way, you don't have to believe that Columbus discovered America, or at least he was credited with it.

Reading about Jesus in the Bible gave me a very clear picture of what a Christian was supposed to be like. I imagine a Christian to be humble; people surrounding this person ask for healing, and he/she would act and heal the person. I saw this Christ-like person teaching me how to believe and how to have faith. Trust God will deliver in Jesus's name. This Christ-like person would forgive his enemies. In my mind, a Christian was a superhuman with powers of prophecies, healing, and love for all. I could not wait to meet a Christian.

I was enjoying the winter in Brisbane, working, making friends, and finally, I knew who the "Son of Man" was. The glorious winter days of Brisbane completed the picture of my new life.

Part 2

Chapter Four – Finding a Church

I and two of my friends left the hostel for a three-unit bedroom at St Lucia, a posh area in Brisbane. Although I got married before I came to Australia, we did not have enough time to complete the paperwork to come as a couple, so I came as a single person. Also, I was testing the waters in this new country. Single people only had a limited time to stay in the migrant hostel, and because of that, my friends and I needed to find alternative accommodation.

By that time, we were settled in permanent jobs and had cars and some savings. St Lucia was a very welcoming suburb, leafy, quiet, and handy to the central business area of Brisbane. All this, coupled with the sunny Brisbane weather, was very pleasant. We missed the effervescent social life of the hostel, though.

My quest to find out about the Son of Man was not completed by any means. I had a question I could not resolve on my own, and I was looking for at least one more answer. Why the name 'Son of Man'?

Every time I drove past a church building, I felt the impulse to stop in order to enquire about this, but I never gathered enough courage.

As fortunate have it, around our unit on Central Avenue, there was a beautiful church building. One beautiful afternoon, I was walking around our new area, and I saw this church; I did not know what type of church it was. To me, all churches were the same.

By that, I mean what particular denomination. I summed up some courage, and I decided to go in and ask my pending question. I walked around the building; it was closed. I never expected a church to be closed, so live and learn, I suppose. The building had large wooden doors, large glass windows, high external walls, and a gorgeous garden to match. The lawn surrounding the church was well-kept and very green.

I could not find a way in, and I could not find a way to contact anybody in the church, so I just went back to the flat, a bit disillusioned.

Other single people had to leave the hostel, too. We were in touch with them through soccer, as a few of us played for the same team.

It happened one Sunday afternoon when I went to visit some of my friends. They lived in a flat in a suburb called Woolloongabba, which was very close to the Brisbane business area. We were all talking in the living room, and our friend El Chico Roberto went to his bedroom. After a while, I noticed that Roberto left the unit, well-dressed and carrying a guitar.

I was surprised and asked my friends what was wrong. Was he upset or something? He didn't say bye or anything?

As a matter of fact, they said, "This guy just goes to the church across the street from here."

This was the first time I heard them talking about him this way. I know they loved him, so I took the 'guy' comment in the context of the 'going to the church' part.

"A church across the street?"

"Yes, just across the street."

I got up and went to see this church. This was my chance at a nearby church, and I knew somebody going there.

I went to the street and looked around. Broadway Street at Woolloongabba was a nice, quiet street with large timber houses on stumps. There were not many trees on the footpaths, but the houses had ample gardens in the front.

There was no church building, though.

I went back in and asked again. They told me again, "Just across the street."

So I went back again.

I could not see a church. There was a larger house than the others across the street. I slowly crossed the street and had a very close look. It was very quiet, and there were some cars in the backyard.

There was a double set of stairs going to a landing that led to a large double door. I kept on investigating, and I saw a bronze plaque on the front wall near the doors. I climbed up the stairs to get a close look. It had an inscription, and it was clear that it was a Spanish Baptist Church (Iglesia Bautista Española.   Later it became Spanish Speaking Baptist Church).

I timidly walked in through the big doors. I heard some soft singing; it sounded nice and melodious.

I sat right at the back near the back wall. For the first time in my life, I was at a church as part of a congregation. I meant to sit, see what it was like, and at the end, try to talk to the people in charge of the church to ask them my question.

It looked like a big house from the outside, that was the reason I could not see it. I was looking for what, in my mind, a church looked like, big, angular, with colored windows and ample gardens. As a child, I visited the Lujan Cathedral in

Buenos Aires on an excursion with the school. Also, I should mention that I married in a Catholic Church. I cannot explain this at all, but anyway, I did so, and I knew what a church looked like from the outside and the inside. It was an extremely pleasant surprise that this Spanish Baptist Church was nothing like that.

From the outside, it looked like a large house. Inside, it was adorned with some flowers on the windows' silt, a large vase with flowers in the front of a simple wooden lectern. The walls were painted white; they had a high open raft ceiling. There were two sets of several rows of timber pews. It was very well-illuminated, and the whole setup was warm and welcoming.

A young woman was playing an old-style organ, and the small congregation was singing very reverently. When the singing stopped, the congregation just silently sat and waited.

The minister came out and walked towards the lectern, placed a Bible on it, and started addressing the people there. I cannot remember what the talk was about, but I do remember the pastor talked a lot about people who congregated in a different church.

Years later, I learned that this church had a bigger congregation, but due to a power struggle with another pastor, there was a split. The second group congregated from there on somewhere else.

This is not as bad as it sounds. There are many reasons why churches split up; the result is that churches spread out geographically, and often, they grow in numbers with new members at their new locations.

After the service, I approached my friend and asked him if they sold Bibles there. They gave me one for free.

I started attending the church regularly and reading my newly acquired Bible. This Reina Valera 1960 version was a gem for me.

My wife joined me in Australia in 1975. We lived in a small apartment for a short time. We both worked and attended church on Sundays.

Our plan was to stay in Australia for a couple of years at least as I came as a financially assisted migrant, and one of the conditions was that if I left Australia before two years, I had to repay the Australian Government the money they spent in bringing me here as a migrant. I believe I was one of the last ones to come under that immigration scheme.

Chapter Five - My Conversion

Something very surprising happened to me around that time. I was leaving the factory where I worked when I heard someone talking to me from behind in Spanish. As the person caught up with me, I realized it was the pastor from the Baptist church. That was a complete surprise to me, and I can say that was an important factor in my decision to continue visiting the church.

I liked that church; people were friendly, the pastor worked like a regular person, and our network of friends was expanding.

During one of my first church attendances, I asked the pastor why Jesus was referred to as the "Son of Man," and his reply was simple and to the point.

-   Because He was born of Mary.

In 1976, our first son was born. We moved away from the central district to a public housing 3-bedroom house.

The pastor visited us many times in our new place; he used to come with his wife and older kids. He was very generous in answering my questions.

My questions were simple.

What is the trinity?

He showed me 1 John 5:7

> *7 For there are three that bear witness in heaven: the Father, the Word, and the Holy Spirit; and these three are one. NKJV*

Another of my early questions was about the Sabbath. In the Bible Reina Valera, there were footnotes every time it referred to the Sabbath, and the footnotes read, "This means Saturday." So I asked about the reason for our meeting on Sundays. Again, he simply pointed out that it was because Jesus was resurrected on a Sunday.

The church experience was very good. It provided a solid circle of people, it was a healthy environment, and I got answers to my questions.

However, I did not convert as such. Probably because I did not understand fully who Jesus was and what He did for us. I understood it intellectually, though, but it never got to my heart.

My second son was born in 1978. It was during one his illnesses that I understood the message, so to speak. My son was merely a few months old, and he had fever convulsions. I remember clearly one day in my despair for him. I prayed to God to pass his illness to me as I could not stand watching my son suffer like that. At the instance, I understood, and all I had been reading made sense to me.

I did not convert straight away. It wasn't until late 1979 that I made the decision during one of the pastor's calls to receive Jesus. I walked up to the front of the church, and I declared that I believed in my heart that Jesus died for my sins, and I confessed that I repented and accepted Him as my Lord and Savior.

Chapter Six – Church Life

After I accepted Jesus of Nazareth in my heart and confessed with my mouth in front of the congregation that He was my Lord and Savior, I knew my next step was to be baptized.

Two or three weeks passed since I accepted Jesus, and there were no signs of the pastor baptizing me. I asked myself, why doesn't he want to baptize me? What is wrong with me? Do I have to do something else? The passage that was in my mind was the Ethiopian's passage:

36 Now, as they went down the road, they came to some water. And the eunuch said, "See, here is water. What hinders me from being baptized?" Acts 8: 36 NKJV

I thought to myself, I'm going to call the Pastor and ask him why he doesn't want to baptize me, and if he does not want to do it, I will baptize myself. I was going to go to the river and baptize myself in the name of the Father, the Son, and the Holy Spirit. And I meant it.

So, I called him, and his first reaction was laughter. He explained to me the water of the baptistery needed to be heated up; otherwise, it was too cold, and that incurred a significant electricity cost, so the practice was to wait until more than one person was baptizing to get the most efficient use of it.

So, my Christian walk started with me intending to baptize myself if the pastor didn't want to do it. Not a brilliant start. Eventually, I got baptized. I talked to people about their baptism experience; most told me they felt nothing special. I felt as if a weight was lifted off my shoulders. I don't mean it mystically, but some sort of relief, maybe because I had to ask to be baptized, and I couldn't wait till it happened.

The church life was pleasant enough and very fulfilling. We made friends with other families who attended the church and invited each other for dinners, lunches, and family celebrations. All in all, it was very rewarding. We went out to picnics and outings, met for prayer meetings at different family houses, and all our children played together. We even had a soccer team and participated in the Baptist Soccer Association competition meeting on Saturday afternoons.

The church met on Sunday evenings, and after the service, we had a fellowship routine of coffee, tea, finger food, conversation, and even table tennis. I have no complaints at all about church life; it is simple and straightforward.

We also had prayer meetings. We alternated these meetings in different houses. I enjoyed singing 'coritos' (praising songs), praying for each other, reading passages from the Bible, and sharing experiences.

Our pastor and the elders were very proactive in relation to church activities. Sometimes, he invited people from other churches to preach in our church and to share the Word. There were theater activities and a choir for the youth of the church. All in all, for a small family church, I believe it was very active.

Somehow, during this period, I thought I should go back to Argentina to share my experience. I thought that in Argentina, people needed to know about the Gospel. Somebody told me that I needed to prepare myself before going there. It was suggested to me that the Baptist Seminary at Mitchelton Brisbane was an excellent place to train myself. I did apply, and I was accepted. It never happened, though.

Also, during this time, my mother visited us from Argentina. She wanted to meet her grandkids. She came with us everywhere, including the church. One day, in one of those 'calling to receive Jesus' days, my mother got up and started walking. I thought she was going to the bathroom. I was wrong. She walked right to the front of the church next to the pastor and shouted that she wanted to receive Jesus

Christ as her Savior. I was astounded; I could not believe what I saw. She got baptized, got a Bible, and participated in every church activity we went to, including the prayer meetings right up to when she returned to Argentina.

They say the Lord acts in mysterious ways. Well, yeah.

Later, I discovered that she congregated in an Iglesia de Cristo church upon returning to Argentina. She and seven other older women did not like it there. They got together and hired a Baptist pastor to help them. Last I heard, that group became a two hundred people Baptist Church in Villa Dominico, Buenos Aires.

The lesson is: if you don't follow God's suggestion, He will find somebody else that will.

Church life was ideal for bringing up a family: healthy lifestyle, positive Biblical teachings, and good people to be surrounded by. In retrospect, I wish that had never changed for my family and me.

Chapter Seven– My Religious Confusion

My understanding of the Christian world was composed of Protestants and Catholics. I did not have a clue what really was waiting for me.

My first religious shock came about when a friend of mine, a Christian, visited the Baptist church we attended. I clearly remember that the pastor was in the middle of a sermon, and my friend stood up and started shouting at the pastor, accusing him of teaching lies. She was very emotional and loud. That is how I discovered the 'Adventists.'

My first theological lesson from that was that Christendom is not as homogeneous as I thought.

My second shock or perplexity, really, was that I noticed the pastor of our church changed the teachings of his sermons according to the books he was reading at the time. I really like that he devoted himself to learning, studying, and expanding his understanding. He always mentioned the names of the authors and gave them credit. I could not discern one way or the other whether the topics were biblical or not, as I did not know enough, but I appreciated him sharing his knowledge.

My third theological lesson was that there were Christian books available somewhere. Who would have thought you needed books to learn about God??? To tell you the truth, I thought he had access to books because he was a pastor. That is how little I knew.

My fourth shock and this was a shock, was when a friend of mine invited me to visit the church where he and his family were congregating. It was the biggest church I could imagine, around three thousand people. I could barely see the preacher from the back. My friend said that it was OK because after the service, they meet in smaller groups. That we did, we got together, held hands, and they started shouting, mumbling sounds. I thought they were doing speech exercises as mostly the sounds resembled speech exercises actors did before going on stage. I remember my sons looked at me with a very inquisitive look on their faces as if asking what was going on. I looked at my wife, and she looked at me. We got out of there in a hurry. That is how I discovered the "Pentecostals."

My learning curve was getting really 'curved.'

Once, I asked our pastor the meaning of the beast in Revelation 17. The answer was once again simple and to the point.'

- The Roman Catholic Church. The seven hills or mountains represent Rome, and the description of the colors represents the color of the robes they use. He also told me that the Catholic Church called Protestants "Heretics."

On one occasion, the pastor and the elders invited a couple of evangelists from New Mexico, USA. They preached and worshiped in Spanish. They were very proficient musicians and singers, and their 'coritos' were really full of dynamism.

They spent about ten days in Brisbane; families took turns having them as guests for lunches and dinner. One family volunteered to host as guests at their home.

It was a great experience and not at all the type of services we were used to have. On their last day, they asked if we wanted to receive the Holy Spirit. The congregation made a queue in the center aisle and, one by one, started parading towards them. Both evangelists laid their hands very gently on people's heads and said something like, 'Receive the Holy Spirit in the name of the Father, the Son, and the Holy Spirit,' and people just went back to their seats.

I just followed everybody and joined the queue. I wasn't sure what it all meant, but I just followed suit. The American evangelists placed their hands ever so gently on my head and said, "Receive the Holy Spirit in the name of the Father, The Son, and the Holy Spirit." I started walking back towards my seat like everybody else. I walked about four or five paces, and I fell on my knees; I lifted my hands to Heaven, opened my mouth, and started to speak in tongues. I did not know what was happening. In the church, we talked about the day of Pentecost and about 'revivals,' but I never expected to live through one.

Our visitors returned to the USA, and our church was never the same again. We became 'Baptist Charismatics.' I know this label was and is not everybody's cup of tea, but there is nothing better if we go by the doctrines and dogmas of man. It is a good thing Our Father does not go by them.

Many events happened in and out of our church.

I started to get more acquainted with the different doctrines of men. I watched some religious TV programs, and I bought some books. Confusion ensued.

Three Gods in one God or just one God; Sabbaths the day of the Sun (Sunday) or the day of Saturn (Saturday). Pagan festivities are adopted as Christian festivities or good old traditional Jewish festivities. Easter bunnies, Easter eggs, Santa Claus, Christmas trees. Arguments such as the cross was not a cross, hell does not exist, and the devil does not exist (say what??). Demons or no demons, divine healing, or satanic healing. A punishing God that will punish you for eternity or a good rewarding God that will allow you to die forever with no other form of suffering in your death? Jesus is just a man, Jesus is God incarnate, or both Jesus is fully God and fully human (I like this one).

These different theological ideas only scratch the surface of the diversity of theological schools of thought.

Anyway, these conflicting doctrinal views were too much for me, and I stopped congregating. I was "in the wilderness" for a long time. Something very significant, though, I never stopped believing; I claimed in my heart God exists, but He is not the God we hear about in churches. I can tell you this much. I felt very strongly in me that I should not stop congregating, but I did it anyway.

Chapter Eight – In The Wilderness

I call the wilderness a period of my life when I found it very hard to find my path in the world. I wanted a job, a career; I had to look after my family. I had three beautiful kids by this time. I needed solid financial resources. And frankly, I blew it all.

It didn't happen overnight. It took a few years for everything to collapse, but collapse it did.

During this period of time, I divorced, and the divorce brought with it alienation from my friends and my own family (not their fault, though). I was too messed up to set up proper priorities; I did not have a permanent job, just enough money to get by, and no prospects. My friends from the church did not contact me except for the rare occasion when I was contacted by my friend El Chico. He always showed concern for my decision. Eventually, he stopped, too.

I have to say this, even if it sounds like a poor cliché. I always prayed, and even if my faith was curbside bound, I somehow always talked to God in my own manner.

My casual job turned into a permanent basic entry-level government job, and this brought some stability to my life. I pursued a tertiary study related to my new job; I was able to buy a new car, save some money, and somehow see a tiny bit of light at the end of the tunnel.

I tried congregating, but I could not find a place where I felt comfortable.

I watched Christian TV programs; I received some material through some of these TV programs. Nothing really helped me much, but I was always trying to find congruency in the teachings.

A few events occurred during this time. I completed my studies in Information Management – Library studies, I worked as a librarian, I moved to a new place in the west suburbs, I found a job using my new skills for the government, and I got a promotion that took me to the capital city. This involved serious traveling time commuting by train.

Eventually, I came across a Spanish-speaking pastor at a train station from all places. We talked and exchanged ideas; he invited me to his church. It was a family church with a few families; most of them shared the same nationality, and apparently, a couple of those families came at the same time from the same country. It was a Spanish-speaking Pentecostal church. It suited me fine.

I attended this church on and off for a couple of years. I married a Christian lady, and we attended this church together. Unfortunately, this time, my marriage did not last long, and I had a second divorce. Some Christian guy, eh?

Chapter Nine – Congregating Again

This again led to isolation, and very quickly, I stopped congregating in this church. However, this time, it was a bit different. I started congregating in another church. An English-speaking Baptist Church. To me, I was a Baptist. I received a gift that was used for my own private edification in the privacy of my room when I prayed and praised in the name of Jesus of Nazareth in Spanish and in tongues. This is the gift I received previously in the Spanish Baptist church

Sometimes, I met the Spanish-speaking Pentecostal pastor at the railway station, sometimes early in the morning, and sometimes after a long day of work on our return journeys. It was on one of those occasions that something very curious happened. Somehow, we talked about the Sabbath, and he said that Christians did not have to observe the Sabbath, and he showed me:

> *'And He said to them, "The Sabbath was made for man, and not man for the Sabbath. 28 Therefore the Son of Man is also Lord of the Sabbath.' Mark 2:27-28 NKJV.*

See, he said, if you believe in Jesus, you don't have to observe the Sabbath.

I looked at him and said, "But it does not say that."

The pastor looked perplexed, had another look at the verse, and said, "That is the way they teach it."

"Who?"

"Those who study," he confirmed.

That moment was so significant for me.

Every time the pastor read this passage, he read, "Christians don't have to observe the Sabbath," even though the passage did not say that.

The pastor was correct in the overall assertion that Christians do not have to observe the Sabbath because we are under Grace not the Law.

Nonetheless, the occurrence had a deep impact on me.

I meditated about it for days, and eventually, I came to the conclusion that I would need to study the Bible myself. I remember thinking, 'Coming back to congregating, nobody is going to pull the wool over my eyes; I will discover what the Word says to me; I will study it myself.'

Again, life in the English-speaking Baptist Church was rich and comforting. It had two services on Sundays, one in the morning and one early in the evening. Although I did not have much contact with the pastor, I liked his style of preaching. Simple, knowledgeable, and to the point if somehow lengthy.

I made friends; they invited me for lunches and dinners. There was a small eatery that opened on Friday nights, and I was there most Fridays after work. Good food, good company, and very reasonably priced.

I attended one of the home groups, and I became very close to two of the elders there. We used to have long Biblical conversations about different topics.

During one of those meetings, I mentioned that I wanted to study the Bible more deeply. They showed me a couple of books; one was a Biblical Dictionary, and the other was a Concordance. They said I would need those and they told me about a Christian Bookshop where I could buy them.

Chapter Ten – The Christian Bookshop And Expanding Horizons

The Christian bookshop was, I believe, an important source of material for me. There were a couple of franchises with various branches. Quite the syndication, really. The one I went to even had a café shop that served some simple lunches. The bookshop was large and well-illuminated with a variety of materials, monographs, both fiction and non-fiction, DVDs, and both study videos and feature videos. It was well furnished with armchairs, chairs, and reading tables. It was a very comfortable and welcoming store.

I met a couple from the Baptist Church. The first thing the husband said to me was, 'The more books I read, 'the more confused I get.' Not the greeting I wanted to hear. Later on, when I gained more knowledge and experience, I discovered why that can happen.

I perused the various sections. The bookshelves were labeled according to the material they held. That did not help me at that stage. Eventually, I came across a title that I thought was meant for me. "Rick Warren's Bible Study Methods" by Ps. Rick Warren.

I followed the advice given in "Rick Warren's Bible Study Methods" book. This book has several methods outlined in it to study the Word. I decided on the 'Devotional method,' acquired the recommended reference material, and embarked on digging into the Scriptures.

I took notes of the verses quoted during sermons and used them as a starting point for investigation. This was funny sometimes as the sermons quoted passages from the Bible but finished up giving three or four points on 'How to do something' or 'How to be something.' Many times, I thought the pastor or the person giving the sermon could just go to the instructions' points' directly, as the passage quoted did not refer to anything like that at all.

Lesson: there are different types of sermons.

Using the devotional method, I became more 'observant' and sharper in picking ideas from the Biblical texts.

One time, just after our regular home group meeting, one of the guys asked the elders who used to meet with us if they could organize a 'men's study Bible group.' The women had a group, and he thought it could be good to have one for men, too. The elder asked me if I would like to lead the 'men's group.' I objected because I did not know how to go about it, and both my elder friends volunteered to help me. I remember clearly one of them had a copy of 'Sermon on the Mount' by John Stott, a LifeGuide Bible Study booklet. The elders showed me how to use this material, and they trained me on how to conduct the meetings, how to use reference materials, and other tips and suggestions. Also, they came to the 'men's group meetings' to supervise me and coach me later if necessary. After a couple of months, they let me fly solo; I was very grateful for the training.

Part 3

Chapter Eleven – Induced Confusion

From my experience with my friend's pastor, that showed me:

> *"The Sabbath was made for man, and not man for the Sabbath. Therefore, the Son of Man is also Lord of the Sabbath." Mark 2:27-28 NKJV*

I suspected that there were probably more instances where believers would believe what they are 'taught' by the experts about a passage instead of believing the actual passage itself. I decided that for me, this passage meant exactly what it says: 'The Son of Man is also Lord of the Sabbath.' It does not mean we shouldn't look deeper into the passage. In fact, as part of our devotional study, we may feel inclined to study it a bit further.

I came to understand that there could be a problem when somebody teaches an interpretation of the Bible because the person receiving the instruction will immediately associate a passage or an idea with what he was taught. Why is that bad?

In my opinion, this is bad because the person no longer believes what the Bible actually says. The person believes what has been taught as to what has been inferred or deducted from what is actually written in the Bible. If that happens often and with a variety of biblical verses, after a while, the person will believe a series of interpretations and not what the Bible actually says, with the final result that the person believes in a phantom bible of interpretations and not the actual Bible. In my opinion this is what creates divisions; people believe in a series of 'credos' or 'dogmas' or 'doctrines of men' creating a 'ghost Bible' or a 'phantom Bible' a 'Bible of interpretations' if you like. I call this changing the Word of God by stealth.

I am convinced that this is what happens to those preachers and scholars who changed the way they believe. They believe in one type of doctrine and will continue believing the same unless they find a new way to see the doctrine that makes more sense to them.

No wonder we read some warnings about the doctrines of men,

> *"That we should no longer be children, tossed to and fro and carried about with every wind of doctrine, by the trickery of men, in the cunning craftiness of deceitful plotting." Eph 4: 14 NKJV*

> *"Do not be carried about with various and strange doctrines..." Heb 13: 9*

In this case, the author of Hebrews talks about food, but the lesson is the same. As Tim 1:6 says,

"Knowing nothing, but is obsessed with disputes and arguments over words."

And our Lord Himself,

"These people draw near to Me with their mouth and honor Me with their lips, but their heart is far from Me. And in vain they worship Me, teaching as doctrines the commandments of men.'" Matthew 15:8-9 NKJV

We can see that in these three examples, the 'doctrine of men' refers to doctrines related to teaching believers based on scriptures. It does not refer to secular doctrines or philosophical or socio-political doctrines.

These warnings bring to mind this preacher saying that he used to believe one way, and then he discovered it was wrong (according to the new interpretation he came across). He claimed that for ten years, he was teaching the wrong concepts. He approached one of his mentors with this concern, and his mentor told him that recognizing he was wrong was a sign that he was growing spiritually. That sounds fine, but what happened to all those people he taught the wrong concepts for ten years?

Chapter Twelve – Doctrine Of Men

I can't say that I know how the doctrine of men started, and probably nobody can pinpoint exactly the point where a doctrine was gestated. Many will claim that 'God showed them,' while others will explain that such and such doctrine arose as an answer to another doctrine, and others will still say that believers had a particular social or spiritual clarification at one time or another. The truth is that doctrines created by men may have various types of reasons for their existence.

I have my own little theory as to how a doctrine may start. Imagine somebody is reading the Bible and comes across:

> *"Let this mind be in you which was also in Christ Jesus, who, being in the form of God, did not consider it robbery to be equal with God, but made Himself of no reputation, taking the form of a bondservant, and coming in the likeness of men." Philippians 2: 5-7 NKJV*

This person reading this passage may think, "Oh, it says that Jesus was like God. Who else I know that was described as being like God. Actually, Michael means like god." Maybe Archangel Michael and Jesus are the same as both are described as 'like God.'" Then, this person starts looking for verses that support that idea and disregards any verses that do not support that idea. Then, a group of theologians and students of the Word conferred and accepted the concept, and Eureka, there you have the birth of a doctrine of men.

Of course, this is a very crude way to describe the birth of a doctrine formulated by men; however, it is not a completely outrageous scenario.

Since I discovered the doctrines of men, I have wondered how two completely conflicting teachings can arise from the Word of God. For instance, 'Free will' vs. 'Pre-destination.'

Can you believe that I was once told by a pastor that he preached the twenty verses (or thereabouts) in the Bible that support the doctrine of free will, and his friend (a Presbyterian pastor) preached the twenty verses (or thereabouts) that support the doctrine of predestination? Obviously, they preached in different denominations. I called this 'denominational indoctrination.' I came to the conclusion that the only way for two opposite doctrinal views to possibly arise from the Bible is for both parties to ignore those verses that flatten their own doctrinal views. They need to ignore (or rationalize it somehow) those verses that disprove their own doctrines.

By the way, in my opinion, the proposition should be:

"Free Will" versus "Forced Will."

Or

"Serendipity" versus "Predestination"

Otherwise, we are comparing apples and oranges.

In my opinion, doctrinaire teachings will always have that element of 'ignoring' the verses or passages that dispute the created doctrine.

Matthew 24 is a point in case. Some theologians dismiss it, claiming it only applies to Jewish Christians. Other theologians dismiss it, claiming that all the signs described have already happened. The sad truth is that Matthew 24 does not fit with their own doctrinal views of the end times (Scatology), so they had to rationalize it out of existence.

I love all of Matthew 24, but my application lies fundamentally with:

> *44 Therefore you also be ready, for the Son of Man is coming at an hour you do not expect. Matthew 24: 44 NKJV*

I hope when He returns He finds me deep in prayer, studying His Word or giving good testimony and not watching football or worse.

My point is always to study the Bible by yourself and get to your own conclusions so that you can discern better.

The doctrinal battle becomes even worse; consider the doctrines of a-millennium, pre-millennium, and post-millennium. Here, we have three conflicting theories of men regarding the end-of-times prophecies.

Once, I saw on YouTube four biblical scholars who actually represented these divergent points of view. Before they started the debate, they prayed and asked for divine guidance to arrive at the truth. Needless to say, at the end of the conference, the truth remained hidden, or at least they did not agree on one. An Evening of Eschatology – Premillennialism, Amillennialism, Postmillennialism (youtube.com) as of 30/07/2024.[1]

These are extremely well-trained Biblical Scholars. They used all the theological tools available to them. Historical and Literary Interpretation, exegesis, hermeneutics, and whatever else is there for them. It is important to note that scholars swear by these tools as the only way to get proper Biblical interpretation, yet they disagree in their interpretations. Using the same available tools that should

---

[1] An Evening of Eschatology – Premillennialism, Amillennialism, Postmillennialism (youtube.com)

point to one truth, they arrive at different conclusions. This simply means these theological tools are not as reliable as portrayed.

I need to clarify that I respect and admire all scholars who take their time and dedicate their lives to teaching us these things. These scholars are very well-prepared, educated, and extremely sincere in the way they believe.

The Word of God warns that we need to be careful with the doctrine of men, and in that regard, studying the Bible by ourselves is a way to heed those warnings.

Chapter Thirteen – What If You Get It Wrong?

When I share my concept of studying the Bible with other believers, the most common reply is what if I got it wrong?

Well, if we take our previous examples of doctrines of men, we have a fifty percent chance of getting the Free Will vs Predestination debate right. Theologians, denominations, and all kinds of experts are saying to us these are the two main doctrines: pick one, and good luck to you. The chances of getting it right are fifty percent.

In the case of the millennium debate, we have a millennium, post-millennium, or pre-millennium to choose from, which gives us a thirty-three percent chance of choosing the correct one.

If we need to get both the free will and the millennium doctrines right, the chances are even smaller. It will be .5 x .33 = .165

Considering that there is a myriad of different doctrines about different topics, the chances of getting them all lined up correctly are meager.

This is the major reason why denominational theologians try to get their part of the puzzle to line up as much as possible. Some call it harmonizing doctrines. Believe it or not, this process also involves ignoring verses or passages that are related to their theme, but it derails their overall point of view.

But for us, as laypeople, this should really give us the confidence to forge ahead and study the Word by ourselves. If these guys, with all their knowledge, resources, consultation, and whatnot, can't agree on what the truth is (each has their own truth) and fight about it constantly, what do we have to lose?

We study for our edification, we do not want to create a new denomination, and we don't need to claim that we are correct and everybody else is wrong.

If within my study of the Bible, I find something that I think is significant and I share it with other believers, and it is pointed out to me that I did not use the meaning of a word correctly or ignore some important issue and by doing so I arrived at an incorrect conclusion. I thank the person who pointed that out to me, and I try again. I am grateful that I learned something new, and I thank God for it. I don't think

God will get upset with me because I am trying to understand His Word, and I messed it up a bit.

It makes sense that we need to establish certain baselines or terms of reference so that we minimize the chance of 'getting it wrong,' and we also want to follow a consistent and organized approach.

Part 4

Chapter Fourteen - Using Scriptures

Often, you are going to hear or read that you cannot take just one verse as a guide for you or take a verse to teach or illustrate a point. That sounds great. However, I know somebody who did exactly that. Our Lord and Savior:

> *"Then Jesus was led up by the Spirit into the wilderness to be tempted by the devil. And when He had fasted forty days and forty nights, afterward He was hungry. Now, when the tempter came to Him and said, 'If You are the Son of God, command that these stones become bread.' But He answered and said, 'It is written, 'Man shall not live by bread alone, but by every word that proceeds from the mouth of God.'"*

Now, our Lord Jesus did not say, "Ok, I am going to use hermeneutics and exegesis from Deuteronomy 8:3 to see if I can use one verse in this modern case as God spoke these words a long time ago for a problem the Hebrew people had at the time." No, Our Lord used one verse appropriately to reply to Satan to resist temptation.

Note that in this first temptation, Satan uses doubt to present the temptation "If you are." But as soon as Satan saw that Jesus used scriptures to rebuke him, then Satan used doubt "If you are" plus scriptures to tempt our Lord Jesus.

"Then the devil took Him up into the holy city, set Him on the pinnacle of the temple, and said to Him, 'If You are the Son of God, throw Yourself down. For it is written that He shall give His angels charge over you,' and 'in their hands, they shall bear you up. Lest you dash your foot against a stone.' Jesus said to him, 'It is written again that you shall not tempt the Lord your God.' Again, the devil took Him up on an exceedingly high mountain and showed Him all the kingdoms of the world and their glory. And he said to Him, 'All these things I will give You if You will fall down and worship me.' Then Jesus said to him, 'Away with you, Satan! For it is written that you shall worship the Lord your God, and Him only you shall serve. Then the devil left Him, and behold, angels came and ministered to Him."
Matthew 4: 1-11 NKJV

We can see clearly that the issue is not quoting one verse from the Bible, even if it is out of context, but the intention of quoting the one verse. It is very clear that verses in the Bible can be misused as Satan did or can be used appropriately as Our Lord Jesus did.

I believe that quoting single verses from the Bible in appropriate personal circumstances may enable us to rebuke the devil; it might empower us to face difficult situations, or it may give us comfort and solace in times of hardship.

The Bible also teaches us that misuse of the Word may occur using not only one verse but also using the scriptures in general.

Apostle Peter not only defended apostle Paul's writings, but he also considered them as scriptures and warned us:

> *"As also in all his epistles, speaking in them of these things, in which are some things hard to understand, which untaught and unstable people twist to their own destruction, as they also do the rest of the Scriptures."*
> *2 Peter 3:16 NKJV*

In this case, it is clear that the intention of some people is to 'twist' the meaning of scriptures on purpose.

In my opinion, the word 'untaught,' also translated as 'unlearnt' or 'ignorant,' gives a sense that we need to be careful how we read scriptures so that we don't finish up 'twisting' scriptures unintentionally. The word 'unstable,' also translated as 'unsteady,' gives a sense of somebody oscillating back and forth.

Let me revisit the little statistical calculation we had before. This time, I am going to add a few more conflicting doctrines invented by men.

(Free will vs. forced will (predestination) .5x (sleeping until resurrection vs. going to heave straight away vs. going to purgatory in between) .33 x (replacement vs. non-replacement church) .5 x (rupture vs. no rupture) .5 x (millennium vs. premellenium vs. post-millennium) .33 x (three gods in one vs. One God) .5 x (once saved always saved vs. losing one's salvation) .5 x (Jesus God vs. Jesus is just a man vs. Jesus is both 100% man and 100% God) .33 x (Sabbath vs. Sunday) .5 x (women having authority over a man in the church vs. women not having authority over a man in the church) .5 x (saved by faith only vs. saved by works vs saved by faith and works) .33 x (baptism by sprinkling vs submersion vs pouring) .33. For illustration purposes I leave it at this no need to add some of the other conflicting doctrines of men out there.

As a lay believer, my chances of aligning all these doctrines of men correctly are:

(.5) x (.33) x (.5) x (.5) x (.33) x (.5) x (.5) x (.33) x (.5) x (.5) x (.33) x (.33) = 0.000030574

These odds are very small for the layman believer to choose the doctrinal 'truth.' So let us make it simple for them by suggesting the new believer pick just a denomination and hope that it is the one with the real 'truth.' Well, in that case, the believer has 1/41000 chances of picking the right denomination. There are 41000 different Christian denominations today. Remember, they all claim to have the only 'truth.'

The Ultimate Guide: How Many Christian Denominations Are There in the World? - Christian Educators Academy As of 18-12-2023.[2]

In all these conflicting doctrines of men, passages of the Bible are quoted to formulate their own doctrinal position. This prompts the non-believers to claim that the Bible cannot be taken as a reliable source because it is 'all a matter of interpretation.'

---

[2] https://christianeducatorsacademy.com/the-ultimate-guide-how-many-christian-denominations-are-there-in-the-world/

Chapter Fifteen – On Biblical Interpretation

In my opinion, the most significant distinction in Bible interpretation is whether the Bible is to be studied as the inspired, eternal, unchanged Word of God or whether it is studied as just another book.

"All Scripture is given by inspiration of God, and is profitable for doctrine, for reproof, for correction, for instruction in righteousness, that the man of God may be complete, thoroughly equipped for every good work." 2 Tim 3:16-17.

Note that Apostle Paul gave this advice to Timothy in regard to the Word of God and the need to adhere to it as part of the warning regarding the last days, specifically for the man of God.

"But know this, that in the last days perilous times will come. For men will be lovers of themselves, lovers of money, boasters, proud, blasphemers, disobedient to parents, unthankful, unholy, unloving, unforgiving, slanderers, without self-control, brutal, despisers of good, traitors, headstrong, haughty, lovers of pleasure rather than lovers of God, having a form of godliness but denying its power. And from such people turn

away! For of this sort are those who creep into households and make captives of gullible women loaded down with sins, led away by various lusts, always learning and never able to come to the knowledge of the truth. Now as Jannes and Jambres resisted Moses, so do these also resist the truth: men of corrupt minds, disapproved concerning the faith; but they will progress no further, for their folly will be manifest to all, as theirs also was." 2 Tim 3: 1-9

Also, in 1 Tim 4, apostle Paul begins his instructions on how to teach and follow God's Word by warning Timothy that:

"Now the Spirit expressly says that in latter times some will depart from the faith, giving heed to deceiving spirits and doctrines of demons, speaking lies in hypocrisy, having their own conscience seared with a hot iron, forbidding to marry, and commanding to abstain from foods which God created to be received with thanksgiving by those who believe and know the truth. For every creature of God is good, and nothing is to be refused if it is received with thanksgiving; for it is sanctified by the word of God and prayer. If you instruct the brethren in these things, you will be a good minister of Jesus Christ, nourished in the words of faith and of the good doctrine which you have carefully followed." 1 Tim 4:1-6 NKJV

It is very important to note that the advice given to Timothy are warnings to the church concerning the last days.

This tells me that the instructions to Timothy were not just for problems in the church at the time (which they are also addressed, by the way) but, more importantly, for the church in the last days. I ask myself if I am living in the last days, and I emphatically say yes. So because I believe that the Word of God is eternal, I believe the instructions given to Timothy then are just as good for the Church of God today as we are in the last days.

I also believe that God sees the end from the beginning, so modern society, science, and technological advances are not surprises to God. His instructions cover what we need to know for salvation and how to conduct ourselves and His Church even in the last days.

> *Declaring the end from the beginning, And from ancient times things that are not yet done, Saying, 'My counsel shall stand, And I will do all My pleasure," Isaiah 46:10 NKJV*

However, there are those who believe that God didn't anticipate the advances of modern society, and they claim that the Bible was not written with modern society in view. They will argue that at the time the Bible was written, societies did not have advances such as stem cell research, satellites, the internet, genetic engineering, artificial insemination, etc. They do not believe that, for instance, the instructions given to Timothy apply today. They will claim that there is a need to apply certain theological principles to investigate accurately and then derive new instructions to suit modern society.

By using this type of reasoning, they will claim, for example, that the letters of Apostle Paul to the Corinthians do not apply to us today. However, the Apostle Paul says:

"Paul called to be an apostle of Jesus Christ through the will of God, and Sosthenes our brother. To the church of God which is at Corinth, to those who are sanctified in Christ Jesus, called to be saints, with all who in every place call on the name of Jesus Christ our Lord, both theirs and ours: Grace to you and peace from God our Father and the Lord Jesus Christ."
1 Corinthians 1: 1- 3 NKJV.

It appears to me that Apostle Paul addresses this letter to a) the Church at Corinth, b) to those who are sanctified in Christ Jesus, called to be saints, and c) with all who in every place call on the name of Jesus Christ our Lord, both theirs and ours. Some experts believe that these letters and others were written as circulars and distributed to other churches, not only the ones addressed directly.

In my opinion, if you call on the name of our Lord Jesus Christ, you are included in the salutation. Apostle Paul addresses specific problems pertaining to the Corinthians, which may as well be the same problems that affect all who call on the name of Jesus Christ our Lord even today. I call this principle of double application. Apostle Paul addresses the problems of the local churches at that time, as well as the universal church of today and tomorrow. And these are not just prescriptions for the local churches these are God's commands. Apostle Paul says it better than me.

> *"Or did the word of God come originally from you? Or was it you only that it reached? If anyone thinks himself to be a prophet or spiritual, let him acknowledge that the things which I write to you are the commandments of the Lord. But if anyone is ignorant, let him be ignorant. Therefore, brethren, desire earnestly to prophesy and do not forbid to speak with tongues. Let all things be done decently and in order." 1 Corinthians 14: 36-40 NKJV*

Note how Apostle Paul tells us that all his instructions are 'the commandments of the Lord.'

I also believe that every instruction, command, precept, and word in the Bible has a value in the natural world and, more importantly, they have a value in the spiritual realm.

Chapter Sixteen – Literary And Historical Interpretation

As we mentioned before, some experts tell us that the Bible was not written directly for us today. They tell us that there is a need to identify which passages are of a universal nature and which passages are culturally specific, and in order to study these characteristics, there is a need to interpret the Biblical texts.

The most common scholarly method of interpretation is the Historical and Literary interpretation, also known as the Higher Criticism method. This is a rigorous and comprehensive method of scholarly research applied to literary works produced over the years. In terms of Christian theology, the most recognized tools are represented by Hermeneutics or principles of interpretation, and Exegesis, which is the discipline of using such principles of interpretation to Biblical passages in order to determine the author's meaning.

The idea behind this method of interpretation is to discover the original or primitive meaning of the texts within their historical and literary context. It will involve an examination of the text's historical origin, time, place, sources, events, persons, customs, artifacts, authors, and audience, among others. They will also look at the use of the language of the time, text structure and subtext of texts, literary form, beliefs, and prejudices of the time, character descriptions, and the narrative style, etc.

In a way, we are recipients of the benefits of such theological investigation manifested in Biblical study material such as dictionaries, atlases, handbooks, encyclopedias, commentaries, translations, study Bibles, study material, theological summaries, OT and NT surveys among myriads of other similar helpful work. But even with these, the believer has to be aware that some authors may sponsor their own doctrinal of men's beliefs and render this type of material bias.

Here, we come to one of the theological studies' most ironic positions in regard to doctrines invented by men. For instance, those who believe in the 'Free will' doctrine and those who believe in the 'Forced will' doctrine will use the rigorous and 'scientific' hermeneutical and exegetical process method of interpretation, and yet, in the end, they will still disagree. More sadly, one of those (or both) will be wrong even though they used these theological tools of interpretation. That is ironic.

Remember that those who use historical and literary interpretation do not believe that God knows the future. They will say things like 'the word of God does not change, but the world changes,' implying that God never saw those changes.

I am completely sure that God knew about hermeneutics and Exegesis and how they would use them before these theological tools were created.

God knew about the gender roles in the last days before even Apostle Paul instructed Timothy about the last days. That is why I believe the Word of God does not change. It does not need to change. The Word of God accounts for every possible contingency at the time it was written and in the last days. The Word is God's breath with God's full knowledge of what the future is going to bring to the believer, even in modern society. God knew very clearly that the advice to Timothy, for instance, was equally valid in the year 2000. Do you believe in an all-knowing God or a God that does not foresee the future?

The Word of God is not just another book.

How do I know that historical and literary interpretation is not the best spiritual tool of interpretation? Because it departs from the premise that The Bible is just another book and the author did not see 'the end from the beginning.'

For example, suppose some theologians claim that Paul wrote to Timothy addressing local issues of the church at that time. They do their hermeneutics and Exegesis and claim that in those days, the role of women was different; they had little education, no managerial experience, and misbehaved in the church, shouting and asking questions and disrupting the service at that time. So they claim that Paul wrote to Timothy addressing those local church problems.

> *"Let a woman learn in silence with all submission. And I do not permit a woman to teach or to have authority over a man, but to be in silence, for Adam was formed first, then Eve. And Adam was not deceived, but the woman being deceived fell into transgression." 1 Tim 2:11-14. NKJV.*

Some Theologians would claim that today, the role of women is totally different. Today, women are working as CEOs of large corporations; they are business managers, captains of industries, and other similar arguments; they know how to behave in church and do not shout and disturb the service, so it is OK today for women to have roles with authority over men in the church as pastors, elders, and deacons because the role of women in society has changed, and God missed that.

Because these theologians don't believe that God knew about modern society, we are now presented with a choice.

God says,

> *"Let a woman learn in silence with all submission. And I do not permit a woman to teach or to have authority over a man, but to be in silence, for Adam was formed first, then Eve. And Adam was not deceived, but the woman being deceived fell into transgression." 1 Tim 2:11-14. NKJV.*

Or

Men say,

"It is OK for women of today to have authority over men in the church in the roles of pastors, elders, and deacons."

So we have to ask ourselves: "Should I believe and obey God or men?"

I think you know my answer: I believe and obey God.

As another example, you may hear that 'during their captive time in Egypt, the Hebrew people learned about making idols, so God commanded them not to carve images.'

However, today is different, so it is okay to have images as long as you don't bow before them.

We are presented again with the following:

God says:

> *"You shall not make for yourself a carved image—any likeness of anything that is in heaven above, or that is in the earth beneath, or that is in the water under the earth; you shall not bow down to them nor serve them. For I, the Lord your God, am a jealous God, visiting the iniquity of the fathers upon the children to the third and fourth generations of those who hate Me, but showing mercy to thousands, to those who love Me and keep My commandments." Exodus 20: 4-6 NKJV.*

Or

Man says,

"It is ok to have images as long as you don't bow to them."

Again, we have to choose between believing in man or believing in God. Please let us believe God.

In the New Testament, the apostle Paul makes it very clear:

> *"Professing to be wise, they became fools and changed the glory of the incorruptible God into an image made*

like corruptible man—and birds and four-footed animals and creeping things." Romans 1: 22-23 NKJV

I appreciate the effort these theologians applied in learning about society in the past, and I appreciate them sharing that information with me.

But nothing gives them the right to effectively change the Word of God or to negate it in any way.

The reason historical and literary interpretation gained the support of Christian scholars is that from around the 1700s forward, this method had some good results when used in relation to books that were not God's breathed. Homer's book Odyssey comes to mind. The fact that this type of interpretation requires the texts to be frozen (or dead) at the time they were written is the main reason theologians always need to qualify that 'the Bible is not written with modern society in mind.' Frozen at the time the texts were written, it is not the same as the supernatural, eternal, unchanged living word of God.

"For the word of God is living and powerful, and sharper than any two-edged sword, piercing even to the division of soul and spirit, and of joints and marrow, and is a discerner of the thoughts and intents of the heart." Hebrews 4:12. NKJV

Chapter Seventeen – Other Interpretation Systems – Literal And Contextual

Literal interpretation refers to a hermeneutics branch that accepts that the Biblical Scriptures are interpreted to the direct meaning expressed by the grammatical structure and historical context of the text.

An extreme form of highlighting the shortcomings of this type of interpretation goes something like this.

Exaggerated shocking example: A believer opens the Bible randomly and reads:

"I am the door. If anyone enters by Me, he will be saved and will go in and out and find pasture." John 10:9 NKJV

Then, the believer will claim that Jesus is a door. As stupid as this example is, you will be surprised how many times examples like this are used to criticize literal interpretation.

Another infantile example used to criticize the literal interpretation is a believer who has an only son called Isaac, opens the Bible randomly and reads:

"Then He said, 'Take now your son, your only son Isaac, whom you love, and go to the land of Moriah, and offer him there as a burnt offering on one of the mountains of which I shall tell you.'" Genesis 22:2 NKJV

And this believer starts making arrangements to go to Moriah. Really?

Literal interpretation by itself could be misused, as could the more scholastic historical and literary interpretation.

Basically, literal interpretation refers to a 'within' approach to looking at the Biblical texts, concentrating mainly on the contextual relationships of the texts.

Another 'within' approach is the 'allegorical' interpretation, which is completely the opposite of literal interpretation. This approach strives to find hidden spiritual meaning, transcending the literal sense of scriptures. While historical interpretation relies more on a 'without' approach to looking at the Biblical texts, it concentrates mainly on outside variables such as customs, use, cultural understanding of yesteryear, etc.

Another significant aspect of the eternal word of God is reflected in the fact that the scriptures were kept after they served their role at the time they were written. If the recipients of the text understood them to apply only to them, they would have disposed of them afterward.

The recipients understood the Word of God had everlasting value. That is the reason Apostle Paul's letters to Timothy were kept. Imagine somebody received the circulars addressed to Timothy in those days, and this person said, 'These letters are not for us; they are addressed to Timothy,' and threw them away. We would not have them today. I don't think they kept the letters for archival purposes. They knew they were written by Paul, the apostle of the Gentiles, and they found valuable instructions in them, as should we today.

We can also read the Apostle Paul's introduction to Timothy's letter.

"For which I was appointed a preacher and an apostle—I am speaking the truth in Christ and not lying—a teacher of the Gentiles in faith and truth." 1 Timothy 2:7. NKJV

It is clear that even if Apostle Paul addressed some local issues, the general audience was always the Gentiles. By this, I mean if we are not Jewish, we are Gentiles. This applies even today.

Let me illustrate with another example. It is very clear and accepted that the Old Testament is a record of the relationship between God's people and God and the announcement of the King's Saviour. So, we could say that the OT was written for the Jewish people. But Apostle Paul teaches us that those records were left for our benefit.

"For whatever things were written before were written for our learning, that we through the patience and comfort of the Scriptures might have hope." Romans 15:4 NKJV

And

"These things happened to them as examples and were written down as warnings for us, on whom the culmination of the ages has come." 1 Corinthians 10:11 NKJV

Again, something written a long time ago was preserved for us in the last days. These are simple examples of finding meaning within the Word of God for devotional purposes.

Finding meaning within the Word is also called contextual interpretation or Lower Criticism interpretation.

Part 5

Chapter Eighteen – Baselines

This is how I approach the study of the Bible for personal devotion and edification.

1. I believe God knows the end from the beginning, and the Word of God is living and active today.

I believe that God foreknew the future at the time He inspired the Scriptures. I believe God knew all the complexities of the modern society I am currently living in. This includes the role of modern women, scientific and technological advances, modern theological ideas, the minds of people, the fast pace of modern life, and the spiritual standing of people today and beyond. Knowing all that, the Holy Spirit left us a record of instructions and commandments that any nine-year-old child could understand and definitely does not need to be adapted to any 'modern' society or culture.

2. Before starting my Bible study, I pray and ask for wisdom, understanding, and for the Holy Spirit to guide me.

3. I believe the Bible is the inspired eternal Word of God.

This means that I believe the instructions and teachings given at the time the Scriptures were written are in effect today. I know the instructions given to Abraham were specific to Abraham. That is why studying the Bible within its contextual environment is so important for devotional purposes and understanding.

What about the books of the New Testament?

For me, studying all the books of the Bible is a devotional act, not an academic or scholarly pursuit.

How do I know if the teachings of the apostles are for me today or are limited only to the local churches of their time?

I found allusions in the books of the NT to "in the last days," "the Day of Christ," "this age and the age to come," "waiting for the manifestation of Our Lord," "the church of God," "New heaven and new earth," "the Day of Our Lord," 'this world," "the world," "the future," "will raise us up," "His coming," "the Day," "till He comes," "O Lord come," "new creation," "fullness of the times," "ages to come," "all generations," "the last hour," "until the Day of Jesus Christ," "salvation revealed in the last time," "when He is revealed," "the last hour," and many other such allusions.

In my opinion, all the instructions and teachings by the apostles for the born again have the underlying foundation for the believer to be prepared for what is referred to today as the return of Our Lord Jesus Christ or the Triumphant

Return of Our Lord Jesus The Christ. Yes, they addressed the problems, issues, and queries from the local churches in their time, but their instructions, in my opinion, are neither exclusive nor exhaustive exactly because of the underlying theme of us waiting and being prepared for the return of our Lord even today.

Let me illustrate from one of the most dismissed books of the NT, which is 1st Corinthians. The book is dismissed by virtue of the interpretation that the book was written for the Corinthians, and they were immature and carnal. Apostle Paul made it very clear that, indeed, the Corinthians were immature and carnal, so that is no mystery. It is further dismissed by saying that Apostle Paul's instructions regarding using spiritual gifts were limited to them because of their immaturity and carnality and that the spiritual gifts were replaced by love.

So let us have a look.

The greeting I mentioned before.

> *"With all who in every place call on the name of Jesus our Lord, both theirs and ours..." 1 Corinthians 1:2 NKJV*

This tells me the epistle is not just for the Church at Corinth but to all who 'call on the name of Jesus our Lord..."

About the spiritual gifts:

> *"I thank my God always concerning you for the grace of God which was given to you by Christ Jesus, that you were enriched in everything by Him in all utterance and all knowledge, even as the testimony of Christ was confirmed in you, so that you come short in no gift, eagerly waiting for the revelation of our Lord Jesus Christ, who will also confirm you to the end, that you may be blameless in the day of our Lord Jesus Christ."*
> *1 Corinthians 1: 4-9. NKJV.*

The reference "Grace of God which was given to you by Christ Jesus" has to make us think and ask: is that the same Grace I am under today?

The reference "so that you come short in no gift, eagerly waiting for the revelation of our Lord Jesus Christ who will also confirm you to the end that you may be blameless in the day of our Lord Jesus Christ."

Some points to note: the 'short in no gift' quote, of course, includes gifts of ministries and activities (see 1 Corinthians 12). Remember that we have pastors, elders, and deacons as ministries; these are spiritual gifts that did not exist in the OT. Some call them operational gifts. If you ever mowed the lawn in your church, believe it or not, you were exercising the spiritual gift of service. This is how I believe anyway.

This also has to make us ask: am I eagerly waiting for the revelation of our Lord Jesus Christ?

My answer is definitely yes. If your answer is the same as mine, then I have news for you. You are included in the passage.

I love how the spiritual gifts are directly related to 'the revelation of our Lord Jesus Christ' and 'blameless in the day of our Lord Jesus Christ.' At the time these Scriptures were written, the return of our Lord was as imminent as it is today. Hardly a matter of temporary local church problems at that time.

Let us see how Apostle Paul deals with a case of sexual immorality in the local church at Corinth, where a man has his father's wife 1 Corinthians 5:1.

Paul instructs,

> *"Deliver such a one to Satan for the destruction of the flesh, that his spirit may be saved in the day of the Lord Jesus." 1 Corinthians 5:5. NKJV*

This tells me that the instruction is again linked to the Day of the Lord or, as we referred to, the return of Our Lord. It is also interesting to note that even if, in the extreme case, the offender dies, his spirit is saved. Some argue that in 2 Corinthians, there is an allusion that this person repented.

Is it true that the spiritual gifts were replaced by love?

Let us see how Apostle Paul introduces love (agape).

> *"Now you are the body of Christ, and members individually. And God has appointed these in the church: first apostles, second prophets, third teachers, after that miracles, then gifts of healings, helps, administrations, varieties of tongues. Are all apostles? Are all prophets? Are all teachers? Are all workers of miracles? Do all have gifts of healing? Do all speak with tongues? Do all interpret? But earnestly desire the best gifts. And yet I show you a more excellent way." 1 Corinthians 12: 27-31.*

Apostle Paul encouraged us to 'earnestly desire the best gifts' and added 'I show you a more excellent way.'

So let us see what "the more excellent way" is.

We can have:

'Spiritual gifts and no love.'

'No Spiritual gifts and love.'

'No Spiritual gifts and no love.'

'Spiritual gifts and love.'

Which is the 'more excellent way?'

In my opinion, 'the more excellent way' refers to the combination of spiritual gifts and love.

Then, Apostle Paul goes into great detail in chapter 13, describing love (agape).

Furthermore, if somebody today thinks that they are so mature in Christ and so spiritual that they do not need the advice given to the Corinthians, well, I do not know what to say to that.

But if the spiritual gifts were only for the Corinthians at that time, why would Apostle Paul write this to the Romans in regard to spiritual gifts?

> *"For as we have many members in one body, but all the members do not have the same function, so we, being many, are one body in Christ, and individually members of one another. Having then gifts differing according to the grace that is given to us, let us use them: if prophecy, let us prophesy in proportion to our faith; or ministry, let us use it in our ministering; he who teaches, in teaching; he who exhorts, in exhortation; he who gives, with liberality; he who leads, with diligence;*

he who shows mercy, with cheerfulness." Romans 12: 4-8 NKJV

Apostle Paul does not use as many details as in the letter to the Corinthians but encourages the use of spiritual gifts, extending from prophecy to showing mercy as part of the spiritual gifts and ministries.

Immediately after, he explains to the Romans about Christian love:

"Let love be without hypocrisy. Abhor what is evil. Cling to what is good. Be kindly affectionate to one another with brotherly love, in honor giving preference to one another; not lagging in diligence, fervent in spirit, serving the Lord; rejoicing in hope, patient in tribulation, continuing steadfastly in prayer; distributing to the needs of the saints, given to hospitality." Romans 12: 9-13 NKJV

Again, Apostle Paul reinforces love:

"Owe no one anything except to love one another, for he who loves another has fulfilled the law. For the commandments, 'You shall not commit adultery, you shall not kill, you shall not steal, you shall not bear false witness, you shall not covet' and if there is any other commandment, are all summed up in this saying, namely, 'you shall love your neighbor as yourself.' Love

does no harm to a neighbor; therefore, love is the fulfillment of the law." Romans 13: 8-10 NKJV

Again, all these instructions are linked to the time of the return of our Lord and Savior, Jesus Christ.

"And do this, knowing the time, that now it is high time to awake out of sleep; for now our salvation is nearer than when we first believed. The night is far spent; the day is at hand. Therefore, let us cast off the works of darkness and put on the armor of light." Romans 13: 11-12 NKJV

We should ask: is the day at hand?

I say it is.

Also, look at what Apostle Paul says in the book to the Ephesians regarding spiritual gifts.

"But to each one of us grace was given according to the measure of Christ's gift. Therefore, He says, 'When He ascended on high, He led captivity captive. And gave gifts to men.' (Now this, "He ascended"—what does it mean but that He also first descended into the lower parts of the earth? He who descended is also the One who ascended far above all the heavens that He might fill all things.) And He Himself gave some to be apostles, some prophets, some evangelists, and some pastors and

teachers, for the equipping of the saints for the work of ministry, for the edifying of the body of Christ, till we all come to the unity of the faith and of the knowledge of the Son of God, to a perfect man, to the measure of the stature of the fullness of Christ." Ephesians 4: 1-13 NKJV

Again, the spiritual gifts are directly referred to as 'the work of the ministry for the edifying of the body of Christ.'

And again, the spiritual gifts are linked to a future, 'till' the knowledge of the Son of God, to a perfect man, and the fullness of Christ. It is very clear that spiritual gifts are not a temporary fix for the Corinthians.

Immediately after this, the apostle Paul talks about love.

"But, speaking the truth in love, may grow up in all things into Him who is the head—Christ— from whom the whole body, joined and knit together by what every joint supplies, according to the effective working by which every part does its share, causes growth of the body for the edifying of itself in love." Ephesians 4: 15-16 NKJV

And again, Apostle Paul emphasizes love.

"Therefore, be imitators of God as dear children. And walk in love, as Christ also has loved us and given

To me, it is very clear the spiritual gifts are for the born-again Christian to be ministered in the body of Christ in love, waiting for the Return of Our Lord and Savior Jesus Christ. Amen.

This is the reason I believe it is a very important baseline to have in studying the Bible as the inspired, eternal Word of God instead of a temporary 'fix' for local churches at the time it was written.

Just to clarify further.

To me, the Biblical times start at 'In the beginning, God created the heavens and the earth' and are completed at 'He who testifies to these things says, "Surely I am coming quickly."' Amen. Even so, come, Lord Jesus! The grace of our Lord Jesus Christ is with you all. Amen.

To me, then, Biblical times are from Genesis 1:1 to Revelation 22:21.

I am in 2023. I am living in Biblical times. Actually, our Lord Jesus Christ says it better than me when He tells His Disciples about the time of the coming of the kingdom.

"And as it was in the days of Noah, so it will also be in the days of the Son of Man. They ate, they drank, they married wives, they were given in marriage until the day that Noah entered the ark, and the flood came and destroyed them all. Likewise, as it was also in the days of Lot: they ate, they drank, they bought, they sold, they planted, they built; but on the day that Lot went out of Sodom, it rained fire and brimstone from heaven, and destroyed them all. Even so, will it be in the day when the Son of Man is revealed." Luke 17:26-30 NKJV.

4. I am aware that I need to allow for literary tools such as allegories, hyperboles, metaphors, similes, parables, anthropomorphisms, narrative, prose, verse (poetry), parallelism, etc. Not only that, but it is necessary to read the section in the context of the verse, passage, and book and to see how it fits within the whole message of the Bible. Hence contextual.

If I read a passage and it is not clear, then I follow a series of little steps that I adapted from various sources. The first three are largely accepted hermeneutical principles, and in my experience, only the first one was helpful for my devotional purpose. I do try to use them all as part of the process. So to the steps then:

5. <u>Scriptures interpret scriptures</u>: I try to find related passages. Generally, I will be using a study Bible, and commonly relevant passages are pointed out. If not, then I may use a concordance or a dictionary. So technically, all the hard work has been done for me.

There are many examples of this in the Bible. For example:

Genesis 3:1 introduces the serpent, and Revelation 12:9 tells us that the old serpent is called the devil and Satan.

Numbers 21: 6-9 Describe how looking at a bronze serpent on a pole saved those bitten by fiery serpents that God sent. John 3: 14-15 explains its significance to us.

Also, the various times the Old Testament is quoted by our Lord Jesus or the apostles in the New Testament are clear examples of the Scriptures being interpreted by the Scriptures.

6. Clear verses to interpret obscure verses.

In this step, I found that most of the time, it is not so much that the verse isn't clear enough; mostly, the confusion arises from having a preconceived doctrinal notion.

For example,

"For it is impossible for those who were once enlightened, and have tasted the heavenly gift, and have become partakers of the Holy Spirit, and have tasted the good word of God and the powers of the age to come, if they fall away, to renew them again to repentance, since they crucify again for themselves the Son of God, and put Him to an open shame." Hebrews 6: 4-6 NKJV.

The verse is clear enough. The text is clear; there is no ambiguity. The first sentence makes a statement, and the rest of the paragraph expands on it.

However, here come the preconceived doctrinal notions of: "once saved, always saved" or "salvation can be lost."

At this stage, those who favor the first notion will readily find those clear verses that support 'once saved, always saved,' and those who favor 'salvation can be lost' will find clear verses that somehow tend to justify their notion.

It does not mean that the verse in itself doesn't deserve special attention. After all, does enlightened mean saved? Is the Heavenly gift forgiveness of sins by grace? What are the powers of the age to come? How can they crucify again for themselves the Son of God? What does fall away mean?

If you are keen enough, you may dissect the verse in manageable parts and, with due diligence and hard work, find a suitable meaning for it all. Theologians particularly had and will probably continue to have a lot of fun with it. Remember that theologians need to tie up everything nicely in regard to their own denominational doctrinal views.

But for me, for my devotion, it just tells me that the people described in the verse are in a spot of bother. My application would be don't join them.

Another example,

> *"Nevertheless, she will be saved in childbearing if they continue in faith, love, and holiness, with self-control."*
> *1 Timothy 2:15 NKJV*

Again, this verse is clear enough. There is a statement, 'she will be saved in childbearing,' and it is extended with some conditions: if they continue in faith, love, and holiness with self-control. Very clear, nothing to worry about. However, it may challenge preconceived notions of salvation.

Preconceived, in this case, means concrete ideas of salvation in relation to verses such as:

> *"And as Moses lifted up the serpent in the wilderness, even so must the Son of Man be lifted up, that*

whoever believes in Him should not perish but have eternal life. For God so loved the world that He gave His only begotten Son, that whoever believes in Him should not perish but have everlasting life. For God did not send His Son into the world to condemn the world, but that the world through Him might be saved." John 3: 14-17 NKJV

I am quoting this verse for illustration purposes only. There are several such passages in the Bible alluding to salvation, and all are related to believing and accepting Jesus Christ as our Lord and Savior.

In fact, John 3: 1-21 develops the principles of salvation very specifically and clearly

Therefore, I investigated further.

When I encountered this verse in my readings, I used all the steps described above.

1- I approached it from my belief that God knows the end from the beginning.

2- I prayed for wisdom and understanding.

3- I approached the verse with the belief that the Word of God is eternal, ie. In effect today.

4- I allowed for literary form, and I looked at the context around it. Verse, chapter, book, the whole counsel of the Bible.

5- I used the 'scriptures interpret scriptures' principle.

6- I used 'clear verses to interpret obscure verses.'

But nothing.

I didn't have a problem with continuing in faith, love, holiness, and self-control. We all have to continue in the faith, practice love, practice holiness, and self-control. Providing, of course, that "continue in the faith" is indeed "continue in <u>the</u> faith."

It was the 'she will be saved in childbearing' that made me curious. Saved here is actually *sōzō*, meaning to save, and the root of *sōtēría*, meaning salvation.

So, I turned to step 7.

7- Principle of first appearance.

The first time ever that childbearing or bringing forth children is mentioned:

"Then God blessed them, and God said to them, "Be fruitful and multiply; fill the earth and subdue it; have dominion over the fish of the sea, over the birds of the

air, and over every living thing that moves on the earth." Genesis 1: 28.

Not specifically to the woman, though.

The first time the 'process' is mentioned specifically and to the woman.

"To the woman, He said, 'I will greatly multiply your sorrow and your conception. In pain, you shall bring forth children. Your desire shall be for your husband, and he shall rule over you.'" Genesis 3:16 NKJV

There is a lot to be derived from this verse, but nothing that would explain to me 'saved by childbearing.' It would appear that before the disobedience, women were already supposed to have pain in childbearing, but the pains were greatly multiplied. It would appear she would not have had pain in the act of giving birth, but God added pain to it. Her desire was not towards her husband, and God changed that also. She was not supposed to be ruled by her husband, and God also changed that. I let the scholars and theologians work all these out.

The first time a messianic consequence of women bringing children into the world is in:

"And I will put enmity between you and the woman and between your seed and her seed. He shall bruise your head, and you shall bruise His heel." Genesis 3:15

For the purpose of establishing study baselines, I don't want to go too deep into any of these verses, but I have to say that a very clear picture is emerging of what 'the women' had to contend with.

Leaving aside for a second that 'woman' is often associated with the Christian Church and for the purpose of seeing this from the gender point of view, we can see that women have a lot on their plate.

a) Direct enmity with the serpent. Who wants that?

b) She is the vehicle to deliver her seed to the world.

c) Her seed is in direct enmity with the seed of the serpent.

d) Her childbearing duties have been negatively affected.

e) Her desire will be towards her husband

f) She will be ruled by her husband.

Here, I can mention that the use of the steps is not linear, meaning that we can move back and forth in order to clarify some topics. For completeness, we could read the announcement and birth of Jesus Matthew chapters 1 and 2 and Luke chapters 1 and 2.

We may pay some attention to the following:

"And having come in, the angel said to her, 'Rejoice, highly favored one, the Lord is with you; blessed are you among women!'" Luke 1: 28.

Could I speculate that the 'she' in 1 Timothy refers to 'blessed are you' and the 'they' refers to 'among women?' Well no. It would not make any sense in 1 Timothy; it does not fit within the context of the verse, and even worse, it does not agree with the whole counsel of the Scriptures. This is the type of danger we can encounter when studying the Bible, and we don't know enough, and we try to be too clever.

This is a warning not to engage in this type of thoughtless speculation. As a devotional act, the best thing to do is not to go beyond what is actually written. We cannot go wrong if we keep within what is written, even if it does not explain everything to us.

Devotionally speaking and for personal edification, we don't need to solve everything. Having exhausted any line of investigation at my level of knowledge, I turned to step 8.

8- Keep it in my heart and wait until it develops more clearly for me.

I still keep this verse in my heart, and I did turn to step 9.

9- Ask, consult, read books, watch instructional videos, and investigate commentaries.

I am very cautious with this step. I need to consider the doctrinal point of view of my source. If I ask a Presbyterian person, I may get one answer, but if I ask a Baptist person, I may get a different answer. The same applies to all types of Christian resources. In mainstream Christian bookshops, you probably will not find Seventh-Day Adventist books, Mormon books, or Jehovah's Witnesses books, and vice versa.

In terms of clarifying 1 Timothy 2:15, step 9 did not provide me with anything significant. I found some exegetic work that bordered speculation more than anything else.

These nine points are what I use as the basis for my devotional Bible study.

Application: I believe the passage as it is actually written. I believe Our Father will fulfill his Word whether my mind understands it or not.

A few words of caution here.

All the definitions of interpretation and methods of study I mentioned before are from a layman's point of view. Strict theological definitions are more elaborated and complex and do not fit in the spirit of this work. It is very clear from my writing that I have no theological training whatsoever. In fact, I was called 'amateur' and 'ignorant' by a couple of people who have. And they are right, of course. So what? Glory to God.

I am not afraid of making mistakes the way I 'interpret' some passages, and not should anybody who wants to expand his/her Biblical knowledge.

In fact, as I mentioned before, when I shared my points of view regarding a passage with my brothers and sisters in the faith, they shared with me some more insightful points of view about the same passage. On those occasions, I go home, revise my notes, and make the necessary adjustments, and I try to find out what caused the shortcomings.

Often, it meant that I did not search deep enough within the scriptures or the material available to me as part of step 9. I am also aware of the law of diminishing returns. This means the more I circle around a topic, the less value for money I will probably get. It is necessary to maintain a balance between too little or casual and too much information, which, in a way, is another problem.

I believe this type of study, although personal, probably works better if taken in groups.

I don't approach my personal Bible study to solve doctrinal differences or to support denominational doctrines. I approach my personal Bible study as an act of devotion for edification purposes.

In fact, I very much go by READ-BELIEVE-ABIDE-WAIT FOR THE LORD as the best way to keep away from doctrinal or dogmatic battles.

Chapter Nineteen – A Practical Example

The baselines are established, and now, how do we make the most of it?

As I mentioned before, I use a system of Bible study that I learned in Rick Warren's Bible Study Methods by Ps. Rick Warren. I adopted the devotional method, also known as the inductive method, or even communal Bible study. Even if you have a more suitable way to study the Bible, going through the following may give you some ideas on how to complement your own system.

I furnish myself with some reference material I use:

NIV Study Bible

NKJV Study Bible

KJV Study Bible

Bible Dictionary

NIV Concordance.

KJV Concordance

I like paper-based material, but all of these, and more, are available in digital format online. I like to write notes and highlight passages on the pages, so my preferred format is paper-based.

I approach the study with the following baselines in mind:

1- God knows the end from the beginning.

2- I pray for wisdom, understanding, and the guidance of the Holy Spirit.

3- The Word of God is eternal and in effect today.

4- I will allow for literary forms, and I will look at the context around it: Verse, chapter, book, and the whole counsel of the Bible.

If the passage is not clear, then I follow with:

5- 'Scriptures interpret scriptures.'

6- Clear verses to interpret obscure verses.

7- Principle of first appearance.

8- Keep it in my heart and wait until it develops more clearly for me.

9- Ask, consult, read books, watch instructional videos, and investigate commentaries.

The Devotional Bible study is based on three simple parts: Observation, interpretation, and application.

<u>Observation:</u>

This part consists of investigating what the passage talks about. I do it by reading verse by verse, asking questions, and noticing statements in it. I keep it as simple as possible.

For illustration purposes, let us look at the Gospel according to Luke.

> *"In as much as many have taken in hand to set in order a narrative of those things which have been fulfilled among us, just as those who from the beginning were eyewitnesses and ministers of the word delivered them to us, it seemed good to me also, having had perfect understanding of all things from the very first, to write to you an orderly account, most excellent Theophilus, that you may know the certainty of those things in which you were instructed." Luke 1: 1-4 NKJV*

Possible observations from the passage:

a) Who is the author?

b) How many accounts were there?

c) What are 'those things which have been fulfilled?

d) Who has taken it into their hands to write these things?

e) What does it mean to be fulfilled among us?

f) Was the author one of the followers of Jesus and the disciples?

g) Was the author one of the Apostles?

h) Is the reference 'just as those who from the beginning were eyewitnesses and ministers of the word delivered them to us' a direct reference to the disciples?

i) In 'It seemed good to me also, having had perfect understanding of all things from the very first,' the author lays down his/her authority to write about them. Not only does the author explain his authority but also his ability to write in an orderly manner.

j) Why would the author go through all the trouble of organizing this account for 'most excellent Theophilus?'

k) Who is this 'most excellent Theophilus?

Having generated some questions, I proceeded to answer them. It is also possible to answer the questions as they are generated. I prefer to list them all as I encounter them because sometimes the answers are given down the passage. If I find the answer down the page, I just go up to the question and annotate the possible answer next to it.

Interpretation (I prefer the term *insights*):

Although the word 'interpretation' is used as part of the process, I like to look at this part as 'gaining insights' or as a 'what can I learn from this' kind of process.

This is step 4 of the baseline points.

A good start at this stage is to 'paraphrase' the passage or to summarise it using my own words.

For example, I would write something like this:

Summary: 'In this passage, the author is describing the qualifications that entitle him to create an accurate orderly record of significant events to inform a very important person while at the same time assuring this person that the account is complete and reliable.'

Then, I would read the context of the passage.

This could be anything from reading the previous chapters or two or three chapters ahead of the passage. In this case, just perusing the subtitles in the Study Bible to the end of the book is sufficient to gain insight as to what the author was alluding to. He does indeed render a detailed record of the life of Jesus Christ.

Answers:

a) From the context, I cannot tell who the author is.

b) From the context, I cannot tell how many other accounts were written. I could speculate that the author was familiar with the other Gospels (Matthew, Mark, and John). I have to be careful when speculating like this. Bear in mind this is an example, and the speculation would remain buried in notes in a box at home. I am just using this as an illustration of how I use this process.

c) From the context, I can venture to say that the birth of John the Baptist was foretold and fulfilled within the text. Similarly, the birth of Our Lord Jesus was foretold and fulfilled. The announcement of the Angels to the shepherds regarding how to find and worship the recently born Jesus was fulfilled; Jesus announcing his death and resurrection was also fulfilled.

d) From the context (verse, chapter, book, overall counsel of the Bible). Again, as in b) I could speculate that Luke knew about the accounts from the Apostles, especially as he says,

"Just as those who from the beginning were eyewitnesses and ministers of the word delivered them to us."

e) From the context, I could tentatively say although the author was not an eyewitness to all of these events, he was a contemporary, and as in point d), it appears he received accounts of events directly. Apart from that verse, I could not find another verse or passage that tells me for certain he was contemporary, but I found certain interesting notes like "Mary (called Magdalene)." he could have said Magdalene, but he clarified the name "Mary" as if he knew the actual person, he also mentioned Joanna the wife of Cuza and Susanna Herod's housekeeper the way he referred about them shows certain familiarity he also says and many other women as if he didn't know them that closely.

These women are mentioned in Chapter 8: 1-3. It does not prove anything about being a contemporary, but it is a good exercise of observation for our devotional purpose. There is another instance in Chapter 2, verse 2, that may be construed as the author's contemporaneity when he writes (This was the first census that took place while Quirinius was governor of Syria). Again, it does not prove anything, but again, it is a good exercise of observation to gain insight into the passage.

f) From the context, I could not answer this question without forcing it a bit. But I could venture to say he was not a disciple or a follower as such, but it seems that he was sort of a 'reporter' in the midst of events. He writes, "All the people were amazed and said to each other…" in chapter 4: 36. Or "large crowds were traveling with Jesus, and turning to them he said…" in chapter 14: 25.

Again, this a small speculation; I could venture to say that it appears he reconciled some accounts from eyewitnesses and some from himself.

g) From the context, I can say that he was not one of the Apostles as he named the twelve, and his name is not there. Chapter 6:12-16.

h) From the context, it appears that some of his contributors could have been disciples, Apostles, and followers of Jesus. Nothing concrete.

Notice I found most of the answers within the Bible. I didn't need to look at resources outside the Bible.

i) I did not write this point as a question. It was just an observation.

j) It appears that Luke knew at least that the Most Excellent Theophilus had been instructed in Christianity and that maybe the accounts he received needed confirmation, as Luke said, "That you may know the certainty of those things in which you were instructed."

k) I cannot answer that question from the context.

Again please notice that most of the answers and observations were obtained from within the text. I did not need outside sources.

The passage is clear enough, so I did not need to use points 5 to 8.

I would need to use step 9 to answer point a) who is the author?

At this stage, I would use my Study Bible as a first port of call. Most study Bibles have an introduction to the books.

My NIV introduction to Luke has the following headings: Author, recipient and purpose, date and place of writing, style, characteristics, source, plan, and outline.

My NKJV Study Bible introduction to Luke has the following headings: a brief statement, author, date, characteristics, structure and overview, Christ in the Scriptures, and outline.

My KJV Study Bible introduction to Luke has the following heading: authorship, date, distinctive features, and outline.

Most study Bibles have a very comprehensive reference system of concordances and footnotes with extra comments and auxiliary study notes, including maps, charts, tables, word study, and cross-reference systems.

In my NIV study Bible, the introduction says that the language and structure of the Book of Luke and the Book of Acts are similar and probably written by the same person. It points out that in the book of Acts, the author uses 'we,' indicating that Luke has been a close companion of Apostle Paul. Also, in 2 Tim 4:11, Paul actually named Luke, saying, 'Only Luke is with me.' This clearly answers question f) from my observations.

To complement the notes in the introduction, I may refer to the cross-reference:

I found a cross-reference in verse 2 with three upper scripts: a) Mark 1:1, John 15:27, and Acts 1:21,22. These don't help me much with answering the questions above, but it completes the picture.

My NIV study Bible has the cross-reference Acts 1:1 just before starting the book of Luke as a subheading that points out to "in my former book, Theophilus, I wrote all about that Jesus began to do and teach…." Acts 1:1.

All these supplementary notes help me get a more complete view of the passage I read.

Why didn't I start by reading the introduction and the reference in the first instance? I am completely convinced that exercising 'observation' of the text awakens a desire to find out more and also sharpens the scrutiny of the scriptures. We become 'sharper' scripture readers.

Also, let me remind you that this is an example of how to go about using the nine steps combined with observation-interpretation/insights-application for the devotional act of studying the Bible.

Now, we can get to the 'application' part.

Application: This part relates to me personally and how I can apply the example of the passage in my Christian life. Sometimes, the passages we study don't have a clear personal application, but the more we approach this system, the more sensitive we become in finding some hints at the practical aspect of the passage.

In this instance, having made the observations and gaining insights into the passage, I get a picture of the devoted person who goes to great lengths to reaffirm somebody that the teachings the person received have very sound and solid backgrounds to the teachings.

My application: I would be sensitive to those who are new to the faith and help them as much as they allow me to. If somebody asks me a question, I would try my best to provide them with an educated answer.

Another example of application: I will keep a network of Christians to exchange information regarding our faith. This could be mentioning new Christian movies, songs, books, educational videos, and videos or recordings of famous sermons, etc.

Create an immediate plan of action. For example, this week, I will call my friend and ask him/her if she/he knows of a good Christian movie.

Another example: I will call the church elders and ask them if I could visit the newly converted believer or the new church member.

Another example: I will invite my church friends to go to the Christian Bookshop to look for study material.

Of course, we do not need to read the book of Luke to know that we need to do those things anyway. However, a reminder never hurts.

Also, the whole exercise was an illustration of how to apply the nine baseline steps combined with the process of devotional Bible Study, namely observation-interpretation/insights-application.

I hope it helps.

Chapter Twenty – Introducing The Template

As I discussed this method of studying the Bible, many brothers and sisters complained to me that it was too cumbersome. I tell them that it may look like that at the beginning, but I assure them that after using the method once or twice, the process becomes automatic. Reading the Bible or checking verses during sermons or lectures, we generate questions and make observations even if we don't write them down. It becomes second nature to discover new insights, and it prompts us to study and investigate further.

I once saw a movie called Catch Me If You Can. This movie is the film adaptation of a book by Frank W. Abagnale and tells his real-life experience as a young con man. In the film, there is a scene where the arresting officer visits the young criminal in jail. When the arresting officer is about to leave, he discloses that he is in a case involving a possible cheque fraud. The young prisoner asked him if he could see the cheque in question. The officer hands Frank the piece of paper, and as soon as this happens, Frank tells him it is a forgery. The weight of the cheque, the thickness of the paper, and the texture of the paper told Frank straight away that it was a forgery.

This skill gained young Frank his conditional release from prison under the supervision of the FBI officer to work for the agency in the fraud division as part of the parole.

By studying the Bible, we should aim to gain enough knowledge and understanding not only for our personal devotional purpose but, most significantly, to detect when charlatans and false prophets try to sell us a fake doctrine. I believe the congregation should know the Bible equally or better than the pastors, elders, and deacons. Also, obeying the Bible goes without saying.

I go as far as saying that if most churches instruct believers avidly in inductive Bible studies, they will do more for Bible understanding and devotion than a hundred sermons.

One way to make the process a bit easier is to follow the steps in the template of Appendix A.

The best way to use the template is to go down the observation column as far as you think necessary, generating some questions, then move to the interpretation/insight column and go down that column, and finally move to the application column going down that column and writing down ideas and summaries.

The template serves as an initial visual guideline. The better you get at this type of study, the sooner you will abandon it or modify it to your own needs.

Part 6

Chapter Twenty-One – Sharing Some Insights

I would like to share some insights I noted by engaging in devotional Bible study. I don't pretend that I 'discovered' anything new or anything like that. These are just examples of using the method and how I developed some applications for my own personal edification. Mostly, they arose from 'observing' the Scriptures more acutely than before I used the study method, and I will not go through each step here or too deep into details. These are just to illustrate some insights.

Example 1: Believing in God an intellectual or a spiritual decision?

"The fool has said in his heart,

"There is no God. They are corrupt. They have done abominable work. There is none who does good." Psalm 14:1 NKJV

Observation

The part that got my attention was, "The fool says there is no God." The word 'fool' denotes a lack of moral integrity. Similar thoughts are conveyed by Apostle Paul in Romans

3: 9-18. The Psalm associates the lack of a belief in God with the corrupt nature of men.

It is interesting to note that the book of Psalms is estimated to have been written between 1400 and 600 BC. This tells me that people didn't believe in God even then. Well before Darwin was born before the theory of evolution was ever thought of, before materialistic theories of all classes were ever imagined, and before science got to the knowledge it possesses today.

People didn't need a theory or an excuse not to believe in God. Why is this? The answer is very simple. Believing or not believing in God is a spiritual matter; it is the basis of the spiritual war. The only difference for the atheists today in contrast to the atheists of Psalm 14 is that today, they can rationalize their unbelief by quoting a theory. Those who don't believe today have a handy, rational excuse. A luxury the unbelievers of Psalm 14th didn't have at that time, yet both their spiritual unbeliefs are exactly the same. There is no difference between not believing with an excuse and not believing without an excuse.

Insight and Application:

I realized that there is no point in wasting time arguing whether evolution is wrong. Carbon dating is not reliable, the Big Bang theory does not explain anything, and there are no examples of DNA gaining information in nature. I came across many verses in the Bible describing spiritual blindness, but I always associated them with the fact that people I met usually gave me the same excuse: 'I believe in science, I believe in evolution, I only believe in what is see' and similar concepts. It wasn't until I saw this Psalm that I realized that believing or not believing in God is a spiritual matter, not a rational matter. My application is that I will still share the Word, but mostly, I will pray for the eyes of the unbeliever to be open to see the spiritual reality of God and His Grace.

I know this is not the greatest insight on the face of the earth, but it was significant to me.

Example 2 – Isaiah 7:14 young woman or virgin?

> *"Now, the birth of Jesus Christ was as follows: After His mother Mary was betrothed to Joseph before they came together, she was found as a child of the Holy Spirit. Then Joseph, her husband, being a just man and not wanting to make her a public example, was minded to put her away secretly. But while he thought about these things, behold, an angel of the Lord appeared to him in a dream, saying, 'Joseph, son of David, do not be afraid to take to you Mary your wife, for that which is*

conceived in her is of the Holy Spirit. And she will bring forth a Son, and you shall call His name Jesus, for He will save His people from their sins.' So all this was done that it might be fulfilled which was spoken by the Lord through the prophet, saying, 'Behold, the virgin shall be with child, and bear a Son, and they shall call His name Immanuel,' which is translated, 'God with us.'" Matthew 1:18-23.

In verse 23, Matthew cites the prophecy of Isaiah 7:14.

Observation: The part that caught my attention was 'all this was done.'

So I asked what does 'all this was done' mean. Therefore, I proceeded to investigate:

a) Mary was betrothed to Joseph, but before consummation, she was with the child of the Holy Spirit.

b) An angel of the Lord appeared to Joseph.

c) The nature of the miraculous conception was explained.

d) The gender of the baby was foretold.

e) The name of the baby was given by the angel.

f) The messianic mission of the baby was explained.

g) His star rose, and the Magi went to worship Him. Matthew 2:1-2 NKJV

Has anything else happened surrounding the time of the birth of Our Lord Jesus?

I found the following in the book of Luke: Chapter 1 and Chapter 2: 1-38.

h) An angel of the Lord appeared to Zechariah in the temple where Zachariah was officiating.

i) The angel announced that Zechariah's barren wife Elizabeth would conceive

j) The angel named the baby John

k) The angel explained the prophetic nature of John

l) The angel explained that John would be filled with the Holy Spirit from birth

m) The angel introduced himself by name (Gabriel) and because of Zechariah's doubted the angel struck Zachariah mute until the birth of John the Baptist.

n) When Zachariah came out of the temple, the people waiting for him knew that a miracle (a vision) had happened.

o) Elizabeth acknowledged the Lord did the miracle of conception for her.

p) Angel Gabriel visited Mary and announced to her she was highly favored.

q) The angel announced to Mary that she would conceive a male child of the Holy Spirit

r) The angel told Mary of her Child's messianic mission.

s) The angel told Mary that Elizabeth, her relative, also conceived because nothing is impossible for God.

t) When Elizabeth gave birth, and Zachariah announced the name of the baby as John, he recovered his voice as foretold by the angel

u) All the neighbors around Elizabeth, Zachariah, and baby John were in awe because all these things were talked about.

u) Zachariah was filled with the Holy Spirit and prophesied of John the Baptist ministry.

v) After our Lord Jesus was born, an angel of the Lord appeared to shepherds in the field announcing a 'sign' to them.

w) The angel was joined by a multitude of the heavenly hosts praising God.

x) The shepherds visited the newly born Child and told everyone around them the events that led them to find and worship the Child.

y) People were marvelled at the account of the shepherds.

z) The Holy Spirit announced to a man called Simeon that he would not see death until he saw the Lord's Christ.

aa) Simeon came to the temple in the Spirit where Our Lord was circumcised.

ab) Simeon prophesied about the messianic nature of Our Lord.

ac) Anna, an eighty-four-year-old prophetess who never left the temple, thanked the Lord and spoke of Him to all who looked for redemption in Jerusalem.

Wow! 'all this' meant that a lot of miracles and supernatural events all around happened to surround the birth of Our Saviour. Prophesies were fulfilled, angels appeared, heavenly hosts appeared, miracles were announced and fulfilled, a virgin conceived of the Holy Spirit, and a star rose to guide the Magi. There were witnesses all around: outside the temple where Zachariah was officiating, the shepherds in the field, the Magi from the east, the people around Elizabeth and Zachariah, and Simeon and Anna.

I asked what it all means in terms of Isaiah 7: 14.

I investigated and found the following:

"Yet this is what the Sovereign Lord says, 'It will not take place, it will not happen. The head of Aram is Damascus, and the head of Damascus is only Rezin. Within sixty-five years, Ephraim will be too shattered to be a people. The head of Ephraim is Samaria, and the head of Samaria is only Remaliah's son. If you do not stand firm in your faith, you will not stand at all.' Again, the Lord spoke to Ahaz, 'Ask the Lord your God for a sign, whether in the deepest depths or in the highest heights.' But Ahaz said, 'I will not ask; I will not put the Lord to the test.' Then Isaiah said, 'Hear now, you house of David! Is it not enough to try the patience of humans? Will you try the patience of my God also? Therefore, the Lord himself will give you a sign: The virgin will conceive and give birth to a son and will call him Immanuel.'" Isaiah: 7: 7-14 NKJV.

This is such a beautiful passage. For the purpose of illustration, I will restrict the observation just to see its relevance to what I observed previously.

<u>Observations:</u>

a) The Lord assures the King of Judah that his kingdom will not be attacked in the near future.

b) This promise is conditional to the King believing the Word of God. Else, he will not be established.

c) In order to make it easier for Ahaz to believe, he is asked, "Ask a sign for yourself from the Lord your God; ask it either in the depth or in the height above."

d) He refused to ask for a sign.

e) The Lord rebukes him and gives Himself a sign. 'Behold, the virgin shall conceive and bear a Son, and shall call Him Immanuel.

At this stage, I am going to use the translation I have on the NKJV study Bible. In this passage, the word 'almah' is translated as virgin. However, it is important to note that Jewish scholars claimed the word 'almah' is used to describe a young woman or a maiden who is physically ready for marriage. In other words, a post-pubescent young woman.

In that case, the passage would be rendered as:

"Behold, the young woman shall conceive and bear a Son and shall call His name Immanuel."

In a simple view, we may ask the question. How is it that a fertile young woman conceiving a child is such a special sign? It really does not appear to be much of a sign.

The answer lies in the significance of 'ask it either in the depth or in the height above' NKJV.

The NIV has: "Ask the Lord your God for a sign, whether in the deepest depths or in the highest heights."

The 1960 Reina Valera has: "Pide para ti señal de Jehová tu Dios, demandándola ya sea de abajo en lo profundo, o de arriba en lo alto." This is my favourite version of this verse.

Regardless of what version we use, the fact is that the scope of the sign is not from this natural world.

I can accept the sign that 'the young woman shall conceive,' but this conception has to be in the context of 'deepest depths or in the highest heights' as established by Our Lord Himself.

Also, notice that the prophecy was fulfilled as Mary was indeed a young woman who conceived a child. The miracle that she was a virgin and that she conceived of the Holy Spirit fulfills the other component of the sign, ie. From the 'highest heights.'

Notice also that the angel did not mention anything about 'virgin.' Mary alludes to it, and the angel makes it very clear without any doubt whatsoever that the conception is very much from the highest height.

"And the angel answered and said to her, 'The Holy Spirit will come upon you, and the power of the Highest will overshadow you; therefore, also, that Holy One who is to be born will be called the Son of God.'" Luke 1: 35 NKJV

In my opinion, the magnitude of the sign was manifested not only in the fact that a young woman who never knew any man conceived of the Holy Spirit, which in itself should be more than sufficient sign of prophesy fulfillment, but also by all the other supernatural events surrounding the birth of our Lord that I mentioned earlier.

The birth of our Lord and Saviour was indeed from the highest height. Amen.

Application/insight: For my personal edification and devotion, the most practical application I was blessed to understand is that I need to believe the Word of God implicitly. Believe and trust Him and His Word without any reservation whatsoever. Ahaz was required to believe the Word of the Lord, or 'he would not be established.' Zechariah did not believe and was rendered mute on the spot. Mary did not understand the angel's words, but she believed and accepted the angel's word. God will fulfill His Word regardless of translations or whether I completely understand it or not. Also, I am completely satisfied with the word 'virgin' in Isaiah 7:14 as I look at it from the point of view that it fulfills a sign from the highest heights.

It may seem a superfluous reminder to believe implicitly, but it is not so, given the constant attempts to dilute, ignore, or substitute the Word of God from both the secular world and from within the Christian world.

A parenthetical break here. I once heard a Rabbi saying that the use of the word 'virgin' in the gospels was the biggest deception in the history of the world originated by Christianity. I have a lot of admiration for the Rabbi who said that as he knows the New Testament Scriptures better than most devoted Christians. He gives us plenty of stick, though, but I can understand where he is coming from.

So this part is exclusively for him (I am sure he will never read this, but I have to do what I have to do). I will be using the term 'Jewish' in the general meaning of Hebrew descent as a narrative tool and not as an accurate theological description. So now:

1- there is not a single hint of 'Christian religion (other than Our Lord Jesus the Christ)' in any of the four Gospels. No one. If the Christians wanted to write something to favor their cause somehow, they would have included something

Christian in it. I don't know a Christmas tree or an Easter bunny here and there (sarcasm). The reason that there is nothing "Christian" in the Gospels is because it was not meant for the Gentiles; it is all written for the Jewish people. Ahaz was the King of Judah, and Isaiah was a prophet to the Jewish people; the sign was for the Jewish people, Mary, Joseph, and the High Priest Zachariah; they are all Jewish, the service in the temple, everything is Jewish. Everything in the Gospel is to introduce the Messiah King to the Jewish people, not to the Gentiles. And it has to be:

"You worship what you do not know; we know what we worship, for salvation is of the Jews." John 4:22 NKJV.

Absolutely, salvation is of the Jews. Glory to God. We Gentiles were adopted later, not a knee-jerk reaction from God, but all part of a plan before the beginning of the Earth. The plan applies to the whole world.

You said that the whole Christian faith was based on the 'corruption' of the Scriptures in Matthew 1:23.

"Behold, the virgin shall be with child, and bear a Son, and they shall call His name Immanuel," which is translated as "God with us." Matthew 1: 23 NKJV

You argued that the Christian faith is based on this verse, and because it says 'virgin' instead of 'maiden or 'young woman,' it is all a scheme.

I am not a theologian, and I am too old and too poor to study this deeper. But please notice the following account:

"Now the birth of Jesus Christ was as follows: After His mother Mary was betrothed to Joseph before they came together, she was found with child of the Holy Spirit. 19 Then Joseph, her husband, being a just man and not wanting to make her a public example, was minded to put her away secretly. But while he thought about these things, behold, an angel of the Lord appeared to him in a dream, saying, 'Joseph, son of David, do not be afraid to take to you Mary your wife, for that which is conceived in her is of the Holy Spirit. And she will bring forth a Son, and you shall call His name Jesus, for He will save His people from their sins.' So all this was done that it might be fulfilled which was spoken by the Lord through the prophet, saying, 'Behold, the virgin shall be with child, and bear a Son, and they shall call His name Immanuel,' which is translated as 'God with us.'

"Then Joseph, being aroused from sleep, did as the angel of the Lord commanded him and took to him his wife, and did not know her till she had brought forth her

Please notice that verses 18 to 19 speak of Mary's condition and the repercussions in regard to her marriage. Then, verses 20 to 21 explain the Divine nature of her condition and tell Joseph how to proceed. We have to keep in mind that this is a record of events that are obviously written after the events by eyewitnesses.

So when Matthew wrote verses 22 and 23, he wrote the culmination of events, i.e., he already knew the condition of Mary and everything else that happened. In My opinion, he wrote the verse as a 'revealed' prophecy intended for the Jewish people, not the Gentiles. I am completely sure at the time, not many Gentiles knew the Scriptures. The same idea applies in those verses where you claim Apostle Paul misquoted the OT. He was writing from a vantage point, prophesies were fulfilled.

Also, even if Matthew 1: 23 verse reads:

"Behold, the young woman shall be with child, and bear
a Son, and they shall call His name Immanuel," which
is translated as "God with us."

In the context of the previous verses, it would still hold true as Mary was a young woman with a child. It just happened that she was a virgin, and the role of the angel confirms the nature of the prophecy in terms of "Ask the Lord your God for a sign, whether in the deepest depths or in the highest heights" in Isaiah. Obviously a young woman with a child would not fulfill the highest heights, would it? But if the woman is a virgin, then it is a completely different story.

Please tell me how many times after Luke 34 there is any reference in relation to the birth of Our Lord in the New Testament. None.

The fundamentals of the Christian faith are based on what was taught to the Jewish people about the Messiah and his Saving role in the world. We Christians believe that Mary conceived our Lord of the Holy Spirit while she was a virgin because it is written, and we consider it to be an important component of the prophetical redeeming role of our Lord Jesus Christ. As part of the whole redeeming prophesy if you like.

But you will be surprised to know that what prevails the most in the Gospels and the rest of the New Testament is His life, His death, His resurrection, and His return.

In the gospels, our Lord Jesus often gave his disciples hints that He had to die and resurrect and the disciples did not understand it. His resurrection is fundamental for us:

"But if there is no resurrection of the dead, then Christ is not risen. 14 And if Christ is not risen, then our preaching is empty, and your faith is also empty." 1 Corinthians 15: 13-14 NKJV

And again:

"Moreover, brethren, I declare to you the gospel which I preached to you, which also you received and in which you stand, by which also you are saved if you hold fast that word which I preached to you—unless you believed in vain. For I delivered to you first of all that which I also received: that Christ died for our sins according to the Scriptures, and that He was buried, and that He rose again the third day according to the Scriptures, and that He was seen by Cephas, then by the twelve. After that, He was seen by over five hundred brethren at once, of whom the greater part remain to the present, but some have fallen asleep. After that He was seen by James, then by all the apostles. Then last of all, He was seen by me also, as by one born out of due time." 1 Corinthians 15:1-8 NKJV

Also:

"And without controversy great is the mystery of godliness, God was manifested in the flesh, justified in the Spirit, seen by angels, preached among the Gentiles,

believed in the world, received up in glory." 1 Timothy 3:16

In fact, some Jewish people accepted the sign and the Messiah and became followers. They were recognized as a Jewish sect called "the Nazarenes" or "The Way." There is no Christian religion there.

> *"Then Saul, still breathing threats and murder against the disciples of the Lord, went to the high priest, and asked letters from him to the synagogues of Damascus, so that if he found any who were of the Way, whether men or women, he might bring them bound to Jerusalem." Acts 9:1-2 NKJV*

> *"But when some were hardened and did not believe, but spoke evil of the Way before the multitude, he departed from them and withdrew the disciples, reasoning daily in the school of Tyrannus." Acts 19: 9 NKJV.*

> *"But this I confess to you, that according to the Way which they call a sect, so I worship the God of my fathers, believing all things which are written in the Law and in the Prophets." Acts 24: 14 NKJV.*

It is all Jewish:

> *"Now those who were scattered after the persecution that arose over Stephen traveled as far as Phoenicia,*

Cyprus, and Antioch, preaching the word to no one but the Jews only." Acts 11: 19.

Then, some Jewish disciples preached to the Gentiles:

"But some of them were men from Cyprus and Cyrene, who, when they had come to Antioch, spoke to the Hellenists, preaching the Lord Jesus. And the hand of the Lord was with them, and a great number believed and turned to the Lord." Acts 11: 20-21

And finally, Jewish and gentile believers in Jesus were called 'Christians.'

"And when he had found him, he brought him to Antioch. So it was that for a whole year, they assembled with the church and taught a great many people. The disciples were first called Christians in Antioch." Acts 11: 26

Notice it says, 'And the disciples were first called Christians in Antioch.'

The point I am making is that it is all about the Jewish, even when great numbers of Gentiles became believers and were accepted as such. Again, it is all about the people of God and their role on Earth as kings and priests (later, the Gentiles also inherited that role). Our Lord is Jewish, the disciples are Jewish, and there is a very important promise to the Jewish people:

> *"Behold, the days are coming, says the Lord, when I will make a new covenant with the house of Israel and with the house of Judah." Jeremiah 31:31 NKJV.*

Our Lord has the Divine duty of confirming that promise to his Jewish disciples.

> *"For this is My blood of the new covenant, which is shed for many for the remission of sins." Matthew 26:28 NKJV*

Apostle Paul, a Jewish man, received the duty of preaching to the Gentiles. (Please read 1 Corinthians: 23-26)

Interestingly enough, the Passover (or the feast of unleaven bread specifically) is the only Jewish festivity Apostle Paul mentioned to the Gentiles in Corinthians to keep.

> *"Therefore let us keep the feast, not with old leaven, nor with the leaven of malice and wickedness, but with the unleavened bread of sincerity and truth." 1 Corinthians 5:8. NKJV*

But that is not all. At the end of times, Jewish people have another important duty:

"And I heard the number of those who were sealed. One hundred and forty-four thousand of all the tribes of the children of Israel were sealed; of the tribe of Judah, twelve thousand were sealed; of the tribe of Reuben, twelve thousand were sealed; of the tribe of Gad, twelve thousand were sealed; of the tribe of Asher twelve thousand were sealed; of the tribe of Naphtali twelve thousand were sealed; of the tribe of Manasseh, twelve thousand were sealed; of the tribe of Simeon, twelve thousand were sealed; of the tribe of Levi, twelve thousand were sealed; of the tribe of Issachar, twelve thousand were sealed; of the tribe of Zebulun twelve thousand were sealed; of the tribe of Joseph, twelve thousand were sealed; of the tribe of Benjamin, twelve thousand were sealed." Revelation 7: 4-8 NKJV.

And now, the cherry on top of everything:

"Now I saw a new heaven and a new earth, for the first heaven and the first earth had passed away. Also, there was no more sea. 2 Then I, John, saw the holy city, New Jerusalem, coming down out of heaven from God, prepared as a bride adorned for her husband." Revelation 21: 1-3 NKJV

Hold on a second, Rabbi. What city? Rome? Not at all; London, not even close; Washington, DC, please. The city is the New Jerusalem.

So, dear Rabbi, there is nothing in the New Testament to substantiate your claim that the use of the word 'virgin' forms the basis of Christian beliefs. We believe the miracle, as did some Jewish people at the time but the focus of the NT was always: His life, His death, His resurrection, and now we wait for His return.

And again let me reiterate, the NT is all Jewish. If you claim that the Gentiles wrote it to advance their cause somehow, well, they did a lousy job.

If you are referring to events outside the Bible then I suggest to you what I suggest to everybody. Stick to the Scriptures, and make your assessments from the Scriptures. We can't go wrong believing the Word of God. End of parenthetical break.

Example 3 – Imprints of the Holy Spirit

> *"As the rain and the snow come down from heaven, and do not return to it without watering the earth and making it bud and flourish, so that it yields seed for the sower and bread for the eater." Isaiah 55:10 NIV*

Observation: I am paraphrasing my observation: 'The rain does not return to heaven until after it does its work in the fields.' This caught my attention

Let me point out that the book of Isaiah is generally accepted that it was written in the 8th Century BC.

Now allow me to tell you a little made-up story.

In the fields of Beersheba, there was a young kid and his father having a conversation. It was early afternoon, and it had just finished raining copiously.

Father - Son, I am going to show you, in a practical way, how they are teaching you lies about God and the scriptures being the Word of God.

Son - How, Dad, how are you going to show me that the scriptures are not the Word of God?

Father- We have seen the rain coming down. Have we not?

Son- Yes, Dad, we have.

Father- Now we are going to stay here, and you will never see the rain going upwards toward the heavens where it came from, as your beloved book says.

Son- I know, Dad, I've seen the rain coming down many times; I've seen the trees and the flowers grow strong because of the water the rain brought down, and you are right, Dad, I've never seen the rain going upwards towards heaven. I often wonder why I have never seen rain upwards.

But even if I don't see it, I believe it because it is written in the Word of God. I also asked my friends and my friends' dads, and nobody has seen the rain 'returning' to heaven, as the scriptures say. But Dad, I believe it all the same.

We can feel a little sad for Junior. His dad passed away sad because he could not get his son to give up his belief in the scriptures. Eventually, Junior passed away, never quite understanding why the scriptures say that the rain returns to the heavens after doing the job of watering the fields when he saw with his own two eyes that it never did. He never stopped believing it, though. He went to the grave believing it. Some people call that 'blind faith' because what the eyes see in the natural seemed to contradict what the spiritually breathed scriptures say. I just call it 'faith.' It is not blind or based on nothing; it is actual faith based on something real, the Word of God.

Isaiah 55 is a beautiful example of what believers in God and his Word call 'imprints of the Holy Spirit.' This means that the Word of God has in it certain concepts spread here and there to show that it was inspired by the Holy Spirit.

In the case of Isaiah 55:10, the concept is that of the water cycle. In the 8th century BC, they did not have any concept of evaporation and its role in the rain cycle. It wasn't until

Bernard Palissy, in 1580, that the concept of the water cycle first came into being. This was not fully accepted scientifically until the nineteenth century.

God wants us to understand that He Knows more than we know, and we should trust Him because of it.

> *"For my thoughts are not your thoughts, neither are your ways my ways," declares the Lord. As the heavens are higher than the earth, so are my ways higher than your ways and my thoughts than your thoughts." Isaiah 55: 8-9 NIV*

Application/insight:

The Bible has many descriptions of events that are difficult to explain. Some may not be for me to know at this stage. We know that our Lord Jesus said:

> *"If I have told you earthly things and you do not believe, how will you believe if I tell you heavenly things?" NKJV 3:12*

The Apostle Paul tells us:

> *"How he was taken up into Paradise and heard words not to be spoken, which no man can utter." 2 Corinthians 12: 4 NKJV*

For some other events described in the Bible, man himself may find the answers in the natural world confirming the Word of God, as in the case of the water cycle around two thousand years after the passage was written.

Again, my application is that I will believe the Bible implicitly and put in my heart any passage I cannot understand at the time.

Just as a reminder.

All these are examples of insights I found using the nine points explained before as part of my devotional Bible study. Here, I presented a summary only, but I did, over the years, go through the Bible in the orderly manner of study before filling hundreds of pages in my notebooks. Of course part of the nine points is to consult material from outside the Bible also. I present some of the insights I gained in this book for illustration purposes only. I teach no doctrine whatsoever other than strongly recommend that each believer study the Bible by themselves and get to their own conclusion by themselves for their own private edification.

The time will come when I will account to my Creator for the method I used to study Bible as well as for everything else I have done in my life.

Part 7

Chapter Twenty-Two

The Bible is a treasure of beautiful verses, passages, and concepts that delight our most inner beings. At this stage, I would like to share some verses that are not poetic as such but are very helpful to me in understanding certain realities. Again please keep in mind that all these citations are for illustration of devotional Bible studies. I came across these verses or passages along my way in devoting myself to scrutinising the Scriptures, and I don't advocate for the readers to follow or to believe them the same way I do. Each brother and sister in the Lord has to do their own Biblical research and arrive at their own conclusions.

a) The Kingdom of God: False Prophets

"The law and the prophets were until John. Since that time, the Kingdom of God has been preached, and everyone is pressing into it." Luke 16:16 NKJV.

To me, this verse acts as a warning. I am very sceptic of people who claim they are special prophets from God. This is particularly true if their message moves away from the Kingdom of God, which is centred on the Gospel of Grace. The only prophets of God, I would believe, are the ones mentioned in Revelation 11 exactly because our Father God told us about them.

> *"And I will give power to my two witnesses, and they will prophesy one thousand two hundred and sixty days, clothed in sackcloth." Revelation 11: 3 NKJV*

I doubt it very much. I will be around on earth to see that.

Application: I will be very distrustful of anybody claiming they are a prophet of God.

b) The killing of Christians: false religions

> *"They will put you out of the synagogues; yes, the time is coming that whoever kills you will think that he offers God service." John 16:2 NKJV*

I love this verse.

In my opinion, this verse is divided into two: the Jewish persecution at the time and the second part extended to "the time is coming," meaning in the future.

Application: Every time I hear or read about the killing of Christians in the name of this or that god, it confirms to me that the Bible is true and that Jesus is Lord. Our Father God saw it coming and told us about it.

c) Him: from above

> *"Then those who were in the boat worshiped him, saying, 'Truly you are the Son of God.'" Matthew 14:33 NKJV*

I shared this verse with some people, telling them that the disciples would have never worshipped a human being; and not only they worshipped Him they also acknowledged Jesus's deity by declaring that He is the Son of God.

They told me that the disciples worshipped Him in Heaven, not Jesus on the boat.

To that response, I showed them:

> *"And He said to them, 'You are from beneath; I am from above. You are of this world; I am not of this world. Therefore I said to you that you will die in your sins; for if you do not believe that I am He, you will die in your sins.'" John 8:23-24 NKJV*

In these verses, Our Lord and Saviour is telling us that He is Him (or He, as you prefer) that came from above, and if we don't believe that, we will die in our sins.

That Jesus is from above is totally consistent with the following:

*"And the Word became flesh and dwelt among us, and
we beheld His glory, the glory as of the only begotten of
the Father, full of grace and truth." John 1:14 NKJV*

Also consistent with:

*"And without controversy great is the mystery of
godliness, God was manifested in the flesh, justified in
the Spirit, seen by angels, preached among the Gentiles,
believed in the world, received up in glory." 1 Timothy
3: 16*

Application: I will defend eagerly the fact that the Word in
the flesh is Our Lord Jesus. I have no doubt whatsoever that
the disciples worshipped Jesus Christ in the boat because
they knew He was Him who came from above.

d) Today – Heaven and Earth as witness

*"Beware, brethren, lest there be in any of you an evil
heart of unbelief in departing from the living God; but
exhort one another daily, while it is called "Today," lest
any of you be hardened through the deceitfulness of sin.
For we have become partakers of Christ if we hold the
beginning of our confidence steadfast to the end, while
it is said, 'Today, if you will hear His voice, Do not
harden your hearts as in the rebellion.'" Hebrew 3:12-
15 NKJV*

I like this passage. I particularly like 'while it is called "Today."

I also like:

> *"See, I have set before you today life and good, death and evil, in that I command you today to love the LORD your God, to walk in His ways, and to keep His commandments, His statutes, and His judgments, that you may live and multiply; and the LORD your God will bless you in the land which you go to possess. But if your heart turns away so that you do not hear, and are drawn away, and worship other gods and serve them, I announce to you today that you shall surely perish; you shall not prolong your days in the land which you cross over the Jordan to go in and possess. I call heaven and earth as witnesses today against you, that I have set before you life and death, blessing and cursing; therefore, choose life, that both you and your descendants may live." Deuteronomy 30:15-19 NKJV*

Note "today" was repeated four times and more particularly: 19 "I call heaven and earth as witnesses today against you, that I have set before you life and death, blessing and cursing; therefore choose life, that both you and your descendants may live.

Application: This is a timely reminder that while there is a "Today" we have the blessing to choose life. Glory to God. Amen.

e) Three in one – which three

> *"For there are three that bear witness in heaven: the Father, the Word, and the Holy Spirit; and these three are one." 1 John 5:7 NKJV*

This is a very interesting verse. Those in the know will tell us that this verse was not found in the early Greek versions of the Scriptures, and that it was added much later.

In fact, I had a Bible which had in the footnotes corresponding to this passage that this verse should not be used to teach as it was added later for some ulterior purpose.

As I don't teach, and I don't say to anybody to believe me but to study the Bible by themselves to reach their own conclusions I am going to use my nine points and try to find out some insights. In fact, I am going to share how I went about it thus:

The Father bears witness –

The Word bears witness –

The Holy Spirit bears witness –

And these three are one.

As this verse does not appear in the NIV, the language 'bears witness' may be confusing. I am going to substitute 'bears witness' with 'testify.' It's not an unreasonable step to clarify the verse. In fact, the Spanish Reina Valera 1960 uses the word 'testimonio. To be fair, the NIV has:

> *"For there are three that testify: theSpirit, the water and the blood; and the three are in agreement..' NIV 1 John 5:7)*

Then my adapted version reads:

The Father testifies –

The Word testifies –

The Holy Spirit testifies –

And these three are one.

My question is: Does this mean that the Father, the Word, and the Holy Spirit are one?

Or

The three testimonies are one and the same. And if so, what is that one testimony?

I expected that the context of the verse in the rest of the passage would answer my questions.

> *"This is He who came by water and blood—Jesus Christ; not only by water but by water and blood. And it is the Spirit who bears witness because the Spirit is truth. For there are three that bear witness in heaven: the Father, the Word, and the Holy Spirit, and these three are one. There are three that bear witness on earth: the Spirit, the water, and the blood, and these three agree as one. If we receive the witness of men, the witness of God is greater; for this is the witness of God which He has testified of His Son. He who believes in the Son of God has the witness in himself; he who does not believe God has made Him a liar because he has not believed the testimony that God has given of His Son. And this is the testimony: that God has given us eternal life, and this life is in His Son. He who has the Son has life; he who does not have the Son of God does not have life. These things I have written to you who believe in the name of the Son of God, that you may know that you have eternal life and that you may continue to believe in the name of the Son of God." 1 John 5:6-13 NKJV*

This text does not expand at all on the idea that the Father, the Word, and the Holy Spirit are one. However, it makes it very clear that the bearing of witness, testimony, or testifying is indeed one and the same.

Please note: 11 And this is <u>the testimony</u>: that God has given us eternal life, and this life is in His Son.

This is what the testimony or the bearing witness is all about. Notice the emphasis: "And this is the testimony". This answers my question; 'and if so, what is that one testimony'?

The next question is when did the Father, the Word, and the Holy Spirit bear witness or testify of the Son?

The Father testifies of His Son:

> *"And suddenly a voice came from heaven, saying, 'This is My beloved Son, in whom I am well pleased.'"* *Matthew 3:17 NKJV*

The Word testifies of himself:

> *"Jesus answered and said to them, 'Even if I bear witness of Myself, My witness is true, for I know where I came from and where I am going; but you do not know where I come from and where I am going.'" John 3: 14 NKJV*

The Holy Spirit testifies of Jesus Our Lord:

"But when the Helper comes, whom I shall send to you from the Father, the Spirit of truth who proceeds from the Father, He will testify of Me." John 15:26 NKJV

This confirms that the three testimonies in heaven are one and the same. The Son of God.

Furthermore, notice the severe consequence of not accepting the testimony and the Son of God.

"And this is the testimony: that God has given us eternal life, and this life is in His Son. He who has the Son has life; he who does not have the Son of God does not have life." John 5: 11-12 NKJV

Please note that this insight arose from my inductive Bible study for my edification and as an act of devotion to study the Bible. I mentioned before that when I asked my pastor about the Trinity, he pointed me to John 5:7

Using the contextual inductive Bible study method, I could not bring in doctrines created by men outside the text of the Bible. I am not trying to prove or disprove the doctrine of men. Theologians with different backgrounds and denominational views are doing a very good job of disproving their counterpart's doctrines, and they are all using extremely complex and scholarly 'literary and historical interpretations, sophisticated hermeneutics, and exegesis. Yet they still disagree. This tells me that their 'scholarly' way of studying the Bible is at least questionable.

Anyway, 1 John 5:7 being a verse so controversial and even nullified, had a lot more to offer than met the eye.

Application: Giving testimony and bearing witness of Our Lord is very significant. What is the best way for me to testify of the Son of God? I think Apostle Paul says better than I could possibly do.

> *"Only let your conduct be worthy of the gospel of Christ, so that whether I come and see you or am absent, I may hear of your affairs, that you stand fast in one spirit, with one mind striving together for the faith of the gospel." Philippians 1:27 NKJV*

f) Light and darkness – Give me light.

> *"And God saw the light, that it was good; and God divided the light from the darkness." Genesis 1:4 NKJV.*

I love this verse.

In the Bible, this verse is a metaphor that indicates the division between good and evil. Right through the Bible, this dichotomy is portrayed as such. But it is also true that God actually made an actual physical line dividing light from the darkness. This line still exists today.

Let me illustrate for you.

Imagine that the sun suddenly dies and it disappears just like that. The last sun's rays will reach Earth in about 8 minutes and 20 seconds, at which time darkness will follow right behind it, engulfing the Earth.

Darkness, as well as the dividing line, also travels at 299,792,458 meters per second.

If it were possible to see this from outside and in slow motion, we would see the light moving toward Earth and, right behind it, darkness.

I imagine that eventually, scientists will discover that as light is made up of photons, darkness is also made of matter.

More fantastically, the reverse is also true. Imagine the solar system without the Sol (Sun), and suddenly, out of nowhere, the Sol appears and starts shining. In that case, the first sun rays will start pushing back darkness till they reach the earth in 8 minutes and 20 seconds.

Every time we turn the lights on in a dark room, this is exactly what happens: the light pushes the darkness back at the dividing line until the whole room is illuminated. If we could see an extreme slow-motion video, that would be what we would see.

"The light shines in the darkness, and the darkness has not overcome it." John 1:5 NIV

"And the light shines in the darkness, and the darkness did not comprehend it." John 1:5 NKJV

Of course, the Word of God is not giving us a class in physics, but as I said at the beginning, the division of light and darkness illustrates the battle between good and evil.

Here, I have to remind you all of what I said before. Believing or not believing in God is a spiritual matter, not an intellectual matter.

"By faith, we understand that the worlds were framed by the word of God so that the things which are seen were not made of things which are visible." Hebrew 11:3 NKJV

I believe that God created the heavens and the earth and all there is by faith, and that is all I need.

Application: In my opinion, this is further proof that God is proving to us that He knows more than we know. To have this physical reality revealed to us around six thousand years ago is astonishing. This insight makes me more resolute to believe His Word implicitly.

g) Trials – faith and believe

"My brethren, count it all joy when you fall into various trials, knowing that the testing of your faith produces patience. 4 But let patience have its perfect work, that you may be perfect and complete, lacking nothing."
James 1:2-4 NKJV

"In all this, you greatly rejoice, though now, for a little while, you may have had to suffer grief in all kinds of trials. These have come so that the proven genuineness of your faith—of greater worth than gold, which perishes even though refined by fire—may result in praise, glory, and honor when Jesus Christ is revealed."
1 Peter 1:6-7 NKJV

Apostle Paul testify of his trials and tribulations, from physical afflictions to the abandonment of his friends and companions during his imprisonments.

We can expect various forms of trials and tribulations to test our faith, but are there any tests that we can do ourselves according to the Scriptures?

"Examine yourselves as to whether you are in the faith. Test yourselves. Do you not know yourselves that Jesus Christ is in you?—unless indeed you are disqualified."
Corinthians 13:5 NKJV

How can we examine ourselves if we are in the faith? Apostle Paul tells us right through his writing that looking at the way we conduct ourselves in the world is one way to see if we are in faith. Practicing self-control, praying, congregating, doing good instead of evil, and living in a way to honour God are good indications that we are in the faith. The contrary would be a clear indication that we are not in the faith.

Trial 1 - How do I know if I believe?

"Later, He appeared to the eleven as they sat at the table, and He rebuked their unbelief and hardness of heart because they did not believe those who had seen Him after He had risen. And He said to them, "Go into all the world and preach the gospel to every creature. He who believes and is baptized will be saved, but he who does not believe will be condemned. And these signs will follow those who believe: In My name, they will cast out demons; they will speak with new tongues; they will take up serpents; and if they drink anything deadly, it will by no means hurt them; they will lay hands on the sick, and they will recover." Mark 16: 14-18 NKJV

I like this passage. Our Lord focused on the spiritual act of believing. He rebuked the disciples for not believing and immediately commanded them to preach to the world, again emphasizing the act of believing and not believing and its consequences.

At the end of the passage, He gave some confirming signs that will follow those who believe.

A word of caution – I believe these signs will actually follow those who believe. Our Lord tells us so. It is important to notice that there may be specific circumstances:

For example,

- 'Casting out demons' I myself would not know when to cast out demons; sincerely, I would not know how to recognize a demon. However, if that particular scenario presents itself (I hope not), then I trust that the Lord will fulfill his Word.

-'They will speak with new tongues.' It is not the case that believers will walk around everywhere and talk in new tongues. That is ridiculous. It will happen when and if necessary for edification purposes and for the Glory of God.

This is hearsay for you, but it is a testimony for me. I have already shared my own experience in this regard. But I would like to share my pastor's experience or at least what he told me. He told me they had a good service at the church on a certain day and that a few believers shared their healing experiences via medicine and prayer. My friend was acting pastor at the time. He told me he felt the edification of the experience and that while recounting the experience in his mind while having a shower, he started talking in 'new tongues' as he called it. He told me he was terrified and stopped it straight away. He told me that was an emotional reaction and not from God, and he stopped it. Even today, I don't know what to say about that.

I recall that on another occasion, we prayed in this church for a 'revival,' but we qualified for it 'but not like the Pentecostals.' Again, I don't know what to say to that. We put conditions on the type of 'revival' we would like.

-'They will take up serpents' No, thank you. Why would I take up serpents? I have enough trouble seeing them through the thick glass enclosures in the zoo.

Having said that, I was on a bush walk in Warwick (a town in Queensland), and a snake bit me. I was walking on a walking trail; a snake was crossing it right in front of me when I saw it. I jumped above it as I could not stop. When I got home, I noticed I was bleeding from my left ankle. I checked it, and I saw two little marks right on top of the ankle bone and blood trickling out of them. I went to the hospital, and they checked me thoroughly and concluded it was not a snake bite; to tell you the truth, this verse did not even cross my mind at all at the time. I know it was a snake, and I know it wasn't green (I have tree snakes in my backyard, even as I am typing this). I am not claiming anything here, but who knows? My account is nothing in comparison to Apostle Paul:

> *"As Paul gathered an armful of sticks and was laying them on the fire, a poisonous snake, driven out by the heat, bit him on the hand. The people of the island saw it hanging from his hand and said to each other, "A murderer, no doubt! Though he escaped the sea, justice will not permit him to live." But Paul shook off the snake into the fire and was unharmed. The people waited for him to swell up or suddenly drop dead. But when they had waited a long time and saw that he wasn't harmed, they changed their minds and decided he was a god."*
> *Acts 28: 3-6 NKJV*

I am guessing that Apostle Paul did not go around picking fights with poisonous snakes. And I am completely sure that I will not. But if it happens, I believe God will fulfill His conditional promise.

-'And if they drink anything deadly, it will by no means hurt them.' We would not know if that has ever been the case with us believers or not. Maybe it happened to us, and we don't even notice it. Remember, not all signs are recognised as in the case of the birth of our Lord. Some recognised the signs, and others did not. I certainly will not drink something deadly on purpose to try this out. I have faith that if that ever happens (again, I hope it never happens to me), the Lord will fulfill His Word. He always has and always will.

-'They will lay hands on the sick, and they will recover' Again. Does this mean I will go to all the hospitals in my area, lay hands on the sick, and they will all recover? No, that is a ridiculous proposition. This sign will be manifested according to God's pleasure when and if necessary. The faith part is to believe so.

How do I know what part of the Bible I should believe?

Very simply. If I believe, "He who believes and is baptized will be saved, but he who does not believe will be condemned." Then I have to believe, "And these signs will follow those who believe," I cannot believe the first part and do not believe the second part. It is not a pick-and-choose proposition.

In my opinion, the test or trial is the act of believing, not the manifestation of the signs. The believing part is from us, and the manifestations of the signs part is from God.

Believing is an important personal choice is consistent with the following:

"Abram believed the Lord, and he credited it to him as righteousness. Genesis 15:6 NIV

And he believed in the Lord, and He accounted it to him for righteousness." Genesis 15: 6 NKJV

"How then shall they call on Him in whom they have not believed? And how shall they believe in Him of whom they have not heard? And how shall they hear without a preacher?" Romans 10:14 NKJV

It is all about believing.

Application: I have to dismiss anything that would make me doubt the Word of God. It is not up to me to decide what part of the Bible I will believe and which part I will not believe. I will believe it in its entirety. I am aware that I will be tested on this. It is a hard trial.

Trial 2-

How do I know if I really love Jesus, my Lord?

"If you love me, keep my commands. And I will ask the Father, and He will give you another advocate to help you and be with you forever— the Spirit of truth. The world cannot accept him because it neither sees him nor

knows him. But you know him, for he lives with you and will be in you." John 14:15-17 NKJV

"For this is the love of God, that we keep His commandments. And His commandments are not burdensome." 1 John 5:3 NKJV

Trail 3 –

How would people know if we are disciples of our Lord Jesus?

"By this, all will know that you are My disciples if you have a love for one another." John 13:35 NKJV

How do we know that we love our brothers?

"By this, we know that we love the children of God when we love God and keep His commandments." John 5:2 NKJV

Trial 4-

How do we know we passed from death to life?

"We know that we have passed from death to life because we love the brethren. He who does not love his brother abides in death." 1 John 3: 14 NKJV

These are just so many tests and trials. We will be subject to various degrees of the testing of our faith.

This is consistent with what Apostle James teaches us.

> *"James, a bondservant of God and of the Lord Jesus Christ, to the twelve tribes that are scattered abroad. Greetings, my brethren; count it all joy when you fall into various trials, knowing that the testing of your faith produces patience. But let patience have its perfect work, that you may be perfect and complete, lacking nothing. If any of you lacks wisdom, let him ask of God, who gives to all liberally and without reproach, and it will be given to him. But let him ask in faith, with no doubting, for he who doubts is like a wave of the sea driven and tossed by the wind. For let not that man suppose that he will receive anything from the Lord; he is a double-minded man, unstable in all his ways."* James 1: 1-8 NKJV.

Some of the trials James tells us:

Economic duress – verse 9. This will have various forms. I am sure we know all about this one.

Temptation – verse 12. Again, we know all about this one.

Discerning the good and perfect gifts from above – verses 16-17. Each of us will know.

Apostle James exhorted us to be doers of the Word, not just hearers of the Word, and summarised it like this:

"Pure and undefiled religion before God and the Father is this: to visit orphans and widows in their trouble, and to keep oneself unspotted from the world." Verse 27. NKJV

"Religion that God our Father accepts as pure and faultless is this: to look after orphans and widows in their distress and to keep oneself from being polluted by the world." Verse 27 NIV

Application: Application I obtained from these trials, I will endeavour to keep the Lord's commandments. I will endeavour to love my brothers in faith. I will find ways to support them, help them, and come to their assistance promptly if required. I endeavour to manifest this love in acts, not just words.

Chapter Twenty-Three – Creating Our Own Values is a no no

I don't need to get too philosophical about defining the word 'values' for believers. I am using the word 'values' to refer to what to believe. Our beliefs will influence our values, the things we come to think of as having worth; our values influence the way we conduct ourselves. And I am convinced that Our Father's Word is the source of all the values we need to live according to His will.

Let us explore how humans can create values that are not given by Our Lord.

"And he received the gold from their hand, and he fashioned it with an engraving tool and made a moulded calf. Then they said, 'This is your god, O Israel, that brought you out of the land of Egypt!'" Exodus 32: 4 NKJV

They made an artefact and assigned it a spiritual value that it never had. They said that the object 'brought you out of the land of Egypt.' This is where believing becomes deceiving. They didn't say, 'believe in this pagan symbol,'. No, they assigned it a value it did not have. They said it was their God. Not only that but once the symbol was presented and believed, then worshiping and offerings followed.

In my opinion, this is the quintessential pattern of idolatry. It is not so much adopting pagan gods and images but assigning Our Lord's divine virtues as value on to them. Notice carefully the process.

They did know about making gods for themselves from their experience in Egypt.

They ask Aaron to make them a god.

Aaron complied.

They made the golden calf but noticed they did not say, 'This is the golden calf from Egypt' or 'We adopt this pagan god as ours.' No, they adopted it as 'their god that brought them out of Egypt.' This is very telling. Pure idolatry would be making pagan gods and worshipping them as pagan gods. There are examples of that in the Bible. However, the fact that they linked this symbol to the act of God taking them out of Egypt is the real idolatry. They transferred God's saving action, getting them out of Egypt, to the golden calf. They created their own value in the form of a metal figurine. They adopted a pagan custom and adapted it to fit God's liberating act.

Aaron did not stop there. He also created another human value: he declared a god festivity.

> *"So when Aaron saw it, he built an altar before it. And Aaron made a proclamation and said, 'Tomorrow is a feast to the Lord.' Then they rose early on the next day, offered burnt offerings, and brought peace offerings, and the people sat down to eat and drink, and rose up to play." Exodus 32: 5-6 NKJV.*

This passage is very detailed.

1- Adopted a pagan image.

2- They claim to believe it was their god.

3- They imputed a value onto that figure by claiming it got them out of Egypt.

4- They invented their own feast for the Lord.

They adopted a pagan image, and they imputed holy values on that image even though it had none. They also invented a feast of their own for the Lord.

Notice what God had to say about it all.

> *"And the Lord said to Moses, 'Go, get down! For your people whom you brought out of the land of Egypt have corrupted themselves. They have turned aside quickly out of the way which I commanded them. They have*

Notice the Lord does not say anything about the playing and
the drinking but the fact that they made themselves an idol .
which they worshipped and sacrificed to, and He specifically
quoted what they said, 'This is your god, Or Israel, that
brought you out of the land of Egypt.' They created their
own values.

As it happened, God already gave them values to follow, and
they didn't need to borrow from the pagan world.

goats. Now, you shall keep it until the fourteenth day of the same month. Then, the whole assembly of the congregation of Israel shall kill it at twilight. And they shall take some of the blood and put it on the two doorposts and on the lintel of the houses where they eat it. Then they shall eat the flesh on that night; roasted in fire, with unleavened bread, and with bitter herbs, they shall eat it. Do not eat it raw, nor boiled at all with water, but roasted in fire—its head with its legs and its entrails. You shall let none of it remain until morning, and what remains of it until morning, you shall burn with fire. And thus you shall eat it: with a belt on your waist, your sandals on your feet, and your staff in your hand. So you shall eat it in haste. It is the Lord's Passover. 'For I will pass through the land of Egypt on that night, and will strike all the firstborn in the land of Egypt, both man and beast; and against all the gods of Egypt I will execute judgment: I am the Lord. Now, the blood shall be a sign for you on the houses where you are. And when I see the blood, I will pass over you; and the plague shall not be on you to destroy you when I strike the land of Egypt.

'So this day shall be to you a memorial, and you shall keep it as a feast to the Lord throughout your generations. You shall keep it as a feast by an everlasting ordinance. Seven days, you shall eat

unleavened bread. On the first day, you shall remove leaven from your houses. For whoever eats leavened bread from the first day until the seventh day, that person shall be cut off from Israel. On the first day, there shall be a holy convocation, and on the seventh day, there shall be a holy convocation for you. No manner of work shall be done on them, but that which everyone must eat—that only may be prepared by you. So you shall observe the Feast of Unleavened Bread, for on this same day, I will have brought your armies out of the land of Egypt. Therefore, you shall observe this day throughout your generations as an everlasting ordinance. In the first month, on the fourteenth day of the month in the evening, you shall eat unleavened bread until the twenty-first day of the month in the evening. For seven days, no leaven shall be found in your houses since whoever eats what is leavened, that same person shall be cut off from the congregation of Israel, whether he is a stranger or a native of the land. You shall eat nothing leavened; in all your dwellings, you shall eat unleavened bread." Exodus 12: 1-20 NKJV

God gave them a very detailed account of a feast and the meaning behind it. Godly values for His people to follow.

It was important for God to perpetuate His saving actions in their memory.

"And you shall tell your son in that day, saying, 'This is done because of what the Lord did for me when I came up from Egypt.'" Exodus 13: 8 NKJV

Notice how God gives them more values to follow:

"So he cried out to the Lord, and the Lord showed him a tree. When he cast it into the waters, the waters were made sweet. There He made a statute and an ordinance for them, and there He tested them, and said, 'If you diligently heed the voice of the Lord your God and do what is right in His sight, give ear to His commandments and keep all His statutes, I will put none of the diseases on you which I have brought on the Egyptians. For I am the Lord who heals you.'" Exodus 15: 25-26 NKJV

Wow! What a beautiful account. God is stipulating to His people the very essence of their relationship. From a simple view, it looks like God talks about 'works,' but the essence is 'faith,' 'trust, 'and 'believe.'

To do right in His sight:

1- Heed His Word

2- Give ear to his commandments

3- Keep all His statutes.

The only way to accomplish these points is to believe that the Lord Our Lord has spoken them, and He will deliver on those words. It is impossible to follow them if they are unbelieving.

God was training His people to understand that only He can save and only He can give them values to follow, and God gave them to understand they were going to be tested. All they needed to do was to believe Him.

It does not stop there. Consider:

> *"Then the Lord said to Moses, 'Behold, I will rain bread from heaven for you. And the people shall go out and gather a certain quota every day, that I may test them, whether they will walk in My law or not. And it shall be on the sixth day that they shall prepare what they bring in, and it shall be twice as much as they gather daily."'*
> *Exodus 16: 4-5*

God tested them, and then He said:

> *"And the Lord said to Moses, 'How long do you refuse to keep My commandments and My laws? See! For the Lord has given you the Sabbath; therefore He gives you on the sixth day bread for two days. Let every man*

God talked directly to Moses and noticed the words, "How long do you refuse?" and also, "For the Lord has given you the Sabbath." I could not find out when God gave Moses the Sabbath, and given the expression 'how long,' I imagined it had passed some time since He did so. I don't know what this means, but I have kept this passage in my heart ever since I first read it. I have read commentaries about it, but nothing is really convincing.

Maybe, and this is a huge maybe, but the answer may be in Exodus 15: "There He made a statute and an ordinance for them, and there He tested them."

The only reason I am speculating (I frown at speculations, but this is to be thorough) is that it talks about 'A statute' and 'an ordinance,' both with undetermined single articles in the English language.

The important point is that God had been training His people for a while to believe and obey Him.

"And Moses went up to God, and the Lord called to him
from the mountain, saying, 'Thus you shall say to the
house of Jacob, and tell the children of Israel. You have
seen what I did to the Egyptians and how I bore you on

189

eagles' wings and brought you to Myself. Now, therefore, if you will indeed obey My voice and keep My covenant, then you shall be a special treasure to Me above all people, for all the earth is Mine. And you shall be to Me a kingdom of priests and a holy nation.' These are the words which you shall speak to the children of Israel." Exodus 19: 3-6 NKJV.

This is such an honour. The Jewish people are so blessed to be called 'a special treasure' to the Lord and to be given the special role on earth to be a kingdom of priests and a holy nation. Also, notice the condition though:

'… if you will indeed obey My voice and keep My covenant, then you shall be a special treasure.' We cannot forget the condition.

As Christians, we are well aware of how serious it is to believe.

"Let not your heart be troubled; you believe in God, believe also in Me." John 14:1 NKJV

And

"That whoever <u>believes</u> in Him should not perish but have eternal life. For God so loved the world that He gave His only begotten Son, that whoever <u>believes</u> in Him should not perish but have everlasting life. For God

did not send His Son into the world to condemn the world, but that the world through Him might be saved. 'He who <u>believes</u> in Him is not condemned; but he who does not believe is condemned already, because he has <u>not believed</u> in the name of the only begotten Son of God. And this is the condemnation, that the light has come into the world, and men loved darkness rather than light because their deeds were evil. For everyone practicing evil hates the light and does not come to the light, lest his deeds should be exposed. But he who does the truth comes to the light, that his deeds may be clearly seen, that they have been done in God." John 3:15-21 NKJV

Some examples of adopting pagan values and giving them some value:

Example 1

"Hear the word which the Lord speaks to you, O house of Israel. Thus says the Lord, 'Do not learn the way of the Gentiles; do not be dismayed at the signs of heaven, for the Gentiles are dismayed at them. For the customs of the peoples are futile; for one cuts a tree from the forest. The work of the hands of the workman, with the ax. They decorate it with silver and gold. They fasten it with nails and hammers. So, that it will not topple.So that it will not topple." Jeremiah 10: 1-4 NKJV

Notice primarily. "Hear the word which the Lord speaks to you, O house of Israel."

And "Do not learn the way of the Gentiles."

Example 2

> *"My people consult a wooden idol, and a diviner's rod speaks to them. A spirit of prostitution leads them astray; they are unfaithful to their God. They sacrifice on the mountaintops and burn offerings on the hills, under oak, poplar, and terebinth, where the shade is pleasant. Therefore, your daughters turn to prostitution and your daughters-in-law to adultery." Hosea 4: 12-13 NKJV*

Example 3

> *"And he sacrificed and burned incense on the high places, on the hills, and under every green tree." 2 Kings 16:4 NKJV*

Example 4

> *"Destroy completely all the places on the high mountains, on the hills, and under every spreading tree, where the nations you are dispossessing worship their gods." Deuteronomy 12:2 NKJV*

Example 5

"Inflaming yourselves with gods under every green tree, slaying the children in the valleys, under the clefts of the rocks?" Isaiah 57:5

Example 6

"Then you shall know that I am the Lord, when their slain are among their idols all around their altars, on every high hill, on all the mountaintops, under every green tree, and under every thick oak, wherever they offered sweet incense to all their idols." Ezekiel 6:13 NKJV.

Again, our Lord is telling us how His people went to the top of hills and made sacrifices under various trees. In Jeremiah 10 and Hosea 4 our Lord goes to great lengths to contrast the values He gives us and the false values adopted from outside His Counsel. In fact, the whole of the Bible is about that contrast.

God didn't tell the Jewish people to adopt customs outside His Word, and the New Testament does not tell us to adopt customs outside His Word.

So, once again. Do we listen to God, or do we listen to man? Do we follow the values given to us by Our Lord, or do we follow the values given to us by man?

Pay attention to this:

I am just quoting a few verses. The truth is that there are more than two hundred references in the Bible about adopting, copying, imitating, following, and creating values outside the values given in the Word of God. They are more easily identified as 'idols, idolaters, idolatry,' and similar terminology.

As mentioned before apostle Paul makes a very clear point about men creating their own values outside the Word of God.

"Professing to be wise, they became fools and changed the glory of the incorruptible God into an image made like corruptible man—and birds and four-footed animals and creeping things." Romans 1: 22-23 NKJV

In my opinion, the same idea of creating values outside the Bible applies to 'doctrines of men.' Let me illustrate:

A new pastor in the church where I was congregating was compiling the church's basic beliefs to put on the church's website. The elders were called to talk about it, and at one stage, the question was raised of whether it was important to put on the website that the church stand on the pre-

194

millennium. There were a few exchanges of ideas focusing mainly on whether that doctrine was a basic belief or just a secondary doctrine. The conversation took a bit of an emotional tone, at which stage it was decided for the most ardent proponent of the pre-millennium to prepare a 'paper' to demonstrate it was a fundamental belief.

I will not continue with the story any further. The important point to remember is that in the Bible, there is no pre-millennium, amillennium, post-millennium, or even millennium, for that matter. Somebody along the way came up with one idea or another regarding the scatological order of the 'thousand years' in Revelation chapter 20, and others then came up with different and contradicting ideas. They created values where there is none, Biblically speaking.

God does not ask us to believe in any of these external values created by men. Men do, to the point that they think it is wrong to adopt their counterpart's theory, and they look at you like your salvation is compromised if you don't agree with them.

The easiest way for me to sieve out manmade values from true Biblical values is to look them up in the Bible. If it isn't written there word for word, I don't have to believe it. In fact, I have to reject them.

Application: as a believer, I have to make sure that I don't fall for images, festivities, religious doctrines invented by man, or customs adopted from the pagan world. As a believer in my Lord and Saviour, Jesus Christ, I don't have to believe in any values (doctrines) created by man. All the values I need are in the Bible, and if they aren't there word for word, I don't have to believe them.

Chapter Twenty-Four – What day is it?

"Now, on the first day of the week, when the disciples came together to break bread, Paul, ready to depart the next day, spoke to them and continued his message until midnight. There were many lamps in the upper room where they were gathered together. And in a window sat a certain young man named Eutychus, who was sinking into a deep sleep. He was overcome by sleep, and as Paul continued speaking, he fell down from the third story and was taken up dead. But Paul went down, fell on him, and embracing him, said, 'Do not trouble yourselves, for his life is in him.' Now when he had come up, had broken bread and eaten, and talked a long while, even till daybreak, he departed. And they brought the young man in alive, and they were not a little comforted." Acts 20: 7-12 NKJV

When I first came across this passage, I asked my first pastor from the Spanish Speaking Church what had happened, as I could not understand the sequence of events described.

My pastor told me that Apostle Paul met the disciples on Sunday morning and preached right through Sunday till midnight. Somebody fell from the window of the upper room, and Apostle Paul assured everybody the young man was alive. Then, early Monday morning, they broke bread, and afterwards, Apostle Paul left. My pastor added that it was the first time the disciples met on Sunday, and from then on, they always met on Sundays. As it happens, I also heard other pastors and preachers making the same claim that from Acts 20, the disciples started meetings on Sunday mornings.

At the time, all I thought was: way to go, Apostle Paul, 24 hours preaching.

Years later, in my early inductive Bible studies, I observed that that passage never actually said 'Sunday.' That caught my attention. By that time, I knew the Jewish people counted the days from evening to evening.

Isn't it funny how we read things but never quite make all the connections?

For example, I read Genesis 1 many times, but I never really saw the significance of every day starting in the evening.

I also came across this verse:

> *"It shall be to you a Sabbath of solemn rest, and you shall afflict your souls; on the ninth day of the month at evening, from evening to evening, you shall celebrate your Sabbath." Leviticus 23:32 NKJV*

So I thought if the Jewish Sabbath goes from evening to evening, It could have been that Apostle Paul met the disciples when the first day of the week started on Saturday evening, preached till midnight, helped the young man that had the fall, broke bread and ate with them and left on Sunday morning.

Still a long, eventful meeting but a little more feasible than the twenty-four hours my pastor told me about. My Baptist pastor was a very good man of God. He was honest and good-hearted, and very dedicated to the Word and his parish. I am in no way implying that his comments were wrong or anything like that. Since that time, I have heard many preachers and pastors that I admire making the same claim that Acts 20 was the first time the disciples met on Sunday morning, and from then on, they continued to do so. I am just emphasising how studying the Bible using the inductive Bible study method may launch us to a Biblical discovery path that is not only a devotional act but could also be fun, instructional, exciting and edifying. At least, that is my experience.

In pursuance of my investigation, I had to corroborate if Acts was written according to the Jewish calendar.

As it happened, verse 6 confirmed it for me.

After confirming that, I used a highlighter to mark every time I found the words 'Lord's Day, the first day of the week, or Sunday' in the rest of the book from Acts 20:13 to Acts 28: 31 in the NKJV.

I expected to find evidence that Apostle Paul or the disciples adopted 'Christian' practices and abandoned Jewish festivities like the Sabbath. In short, I expected to find evidence that, indeed, the disciples met on Sundays, or the Lord's Day, or even just the first day of the week. I suspected that in those early days, there would be a lot of interchangeable practices as Apostle Paul had to contend with the Jewish people following him and trying to convert Gentiles to Judaism as proselytes. So, I expected him to teach and reinforce the new practice.

Apostle Paul found some disciples at Tyre, where he stayed for seven days. Acts 21: 3-4 NKJV. I am sure that within those seven days, there was a Sunday, yet the Scriptures don't mention anything.

At Caesarea, Apostle Paul and companions stayed 'many days' in the house of the evangelist Philip. The duration of their stay there is not clear, but again, no Sunday, first day, or Lord's Day was mentioned. Acts 21: 8-10 NKJV.

On his return to Jerusalem, Apostle Paul and his companions, together with the 'brethren and fathers' would have had many occasions to meet on Sundays if indeed it was the new practice as it was the case when Apostle Paul was in Rome, yet there is no mention of Sundays, the first day of the week or the Lord's Day anywhere in the rest of the book of Acts. I could not find one single occasion where the Holy Spirit would leave a record of such occurrence.

What did happen is that Apostle Paul had to defend his Jewish heritage and customs. He did so successfully, also he was successful in defending his ministry to the Gentiles and reinforcing that Gentiles did not have to follow the Law or Jewish customs.

I did not have to use my highlighter, not even once. I conclude that the idea of the disciples meeting on Sundays came from outside the Bible, particularly outside the book of Acts.

I still find it interesting how common it is for preachers still teaching that the Sunday meetings started during the book of Acts.

I admit that Acts 20: 7-12 could describe Apostle Paul's teaching and preaching from Sunday morning to Monday morning, but I also accounted for the more likely possibility that Apostle Paul taught and preached from Saturday evening to Sunday morning.

This exercise was just a demonstration of the devotional act of studying the Bible using the inductive method. It is not a comment on what day to meet as Christians or anything like that. If we meet for the Lord with faith and love from our hearts, I don't see 'days' as an issue.

Of course, Apostle Paul puts it a lot better than me.

> *"Receive one who is weak in the faith, but not to disputes over doubtful things. For one believes he may eat all things, but he who is weak eats only vegetables. Let not him who eats despise him who does not eat, and let not him who does not eat judge him who eats, for God has received him. Who are you to judge another's servant? To his own master, he stands or falls. Indeed, he will be made to stand, for God is able to make him stand. One person esteems one day above another; another esteems every day alike. Let each be fully convinced in his own mind. He who observes the day, observes it to the Lord; and he who does not observe the day, to the Lord he does not observe it. He who eats, eats to the Lord, for he gives*

God thanks; and he who does not eat, to the Lord he does not eat, and gives God thanks. For none of us lives to himself, and no one dies to himself. For if we live, we live to the Lord; and if we die, we die to the Lord. Therefore, whether we live or die, we are the Lord's. For to this end Christ died and rose and lived again, that He might be Lord of both the dead and the living. But why do you judge your brother? Or why do you show contempt for your brother? For we shall all stand before the judgment seat of Christ. For it is written: 'As I live, says the Lord, every knee shall bow to Me, and every tongue shall confess to God.' So then, each of us shall give an account of himself to God. Therefore let us not judge one another anymore, but rather resolve this, not to put a stumbling block or a cause to fall in our brother's way." Romans 14: 1- 13 NKJV.

"One person esteems one day above another; another esteems every day alike. Let each be fully convinced in his own mind. He who observes the day, observes it to the Lord; and he who does not observe the day, to the Lord he does not observe it."

Theologians and scholars will argue that these verses allude to 'full or new moon' Sabbaths, not the seventh-day Sabbath. They can say that but the Bible does not say that.

Why did I find this interesting? Well, I am amazed at the claim that the book of Acts tells us the disciples always met on Sunday mornings from Act 20 when there is nothing of the sort in the book of Acts. The Book of Acts is believed to have been authored between early AD60 to late AD60. Some scholars think that it is extremely significant the book does not mention the destruction of the Temple in AD 70. Other scholars would like to make its authorship as late as AD 100, and some scholars even try to line it up with catholic developments.

This is the reason point 9 of the study system encourages us to search outside the Scriptures with the condition to be extremely careful as each denominational theologian will try to push their own denominational training.

For completeness, I am including this:

> *"Early Christians, at first mainly Jewish, observed the seventh-day Sabbath with prayer and rest. At the beginning of the second century the Church Father Ignatius of Antioch approved non-observance of the Sabbath. The now majority practice of Christians is to observe Sunday, called the Lord's Day, rather than the Jewish seventh-day Sabbath as a day of rest and worship."*

Apparently, this was part of a letter written by Ignatius around AD 115.

https://archive.gci.org/articles/sabbath-and-sunday-in-the-early-church/ as at 18/03/2024.[3]

Also, I don't want to be disrespectful, but the only Father of my Church is the Lord Jesus Christ.

> *"And I also say to you that you are Peter, and on this rock, I will build My Church, and the gates of Hades shall not prevail against it." Matthew 16:18 NKJV.*

Also, as part of being thorough in applying point 9 of the study method:

> *"On the venerable Day of the Sun, let the magistrates and people residing in cities rest, and let all the workshops be closed." Constantine, 321 A.D.*

> *"The popular complaint against the Christians was- they despise our sun-god, they have divine services on Saturday, they desecrate the sacred earth by burying their dead in it." Truth Triumphant, p. 170, Persia 335-375 AD (40 years persecution under Shapur 11th)*

---

[3] https://archive.gci.org/articles/sabbath-and-sunday-in-the-early-church/

"Canon 29- Christians shall not Judaize and be idle on Saturday. But shall work on that day; but the Lord's day they shall especially honor. And, as being Christians, shall, if possible, do no work on that day." Hefele's Councils, Vol. 2, b. 6. Council Laodicia- 365 A.D.

https://thechristianlife.com/catholic-church-says-to-have-changed-the-sabbath-to-sunday/ as at 18/03/2024.[4]

Notice particularly 'the popular complaints against the Christians,' and that happened around AD 335-375, long after Acts 20. This means that the Christians didn't congregate on Sundays in the Book of Acts.

Application: I will not judge those Christians who congregate on Saturday as I will not judge those Christians who congregate on Sundays. I cannot write an application for others, but I hope I don't get judged because I congregate on Sundays.

---

[4] https://thechristianlife.com/catholic-church-says-to-have-changed-the-sabbath-to-sunday/

Chapter Twenty-Five – I did not want to get into this.

The inductive Bible study method is, for me, a beautiful and edifying act of devotion. I avoid getting involved in discussing doctrines created by men as I believe discussing these doctrines takes away the beauty of studying the Bible as a lay person. As I quoted in the previous chapter, teachings like the Lord's Day and Sunday worshiping were created outside the Bible by men who had their own reasons for doing so, and then I told you I congregate on Sundays now, so I feel the need to elaborate a little bit more on that conflicting position.

I believe Apostle Paul had the authority to teach and correct the Gentiles, so let's see how he handled discussion of food or days of worshiping:

"So then each of us shall give an account of himself to God. Therefore let us not judge one another anymore, but rather resolve this, not to put a stumbling block or a cause to fall in our brother's way." Romans 14: 12- 13 NKJV.

Note Apostle Paul, the Apostle to the Gentiles, did not say let us resolve this by me forcing you to observe this day or that day and to eat this or that. NO! he did not say so, and he was our Apostle.

So my question is: Who are Ignatius or Constantine or anybody else for that matter to override Apostle Paul's teachings? Their names and their councils' names are not in the Bible. Emperor Constantine had the authority of his army, I suppose. To have a Roman army at your disposal goes a long way in the art of persuasion.

As I said before, some people negate Apostle Paul's teachings in Romans 14 by saying that the Apostle was referring to new moons, Sabbaths, and nothing else. I believe that the Holy Spirit knows what to communicate, and Apostle Paul was a gifted writer who knew how to express himself. If that was what he wanted to communicate to us, he would have said so.

Now, the whole premise of writing this book, my thesis, if you'd like, is that I do not have to believe anything written after 96 AD (approximately the time of the completion of the book of Revelation). I have the Word of God in my hand, and it has the complete set of beliefs and values by which I could become a good Christian (long way to go, though). I further argued that I only need to believe what is actually written in the Bible in order for me to achieve that.

So, if I believe my own thesis, I know that congregating on Sundays as Lord's Day was invented outside the Bible and later than the year 96 AD (remember Ignatius 115AD and Constantine 321 AD). How come I congregate on Sundays?

I am glad you asked that question. Let me answer it for you.

a) I am not Jewish.

b) The law was given to the Jewish people. Exodus 19 and 20.

c) As a Gentile (a non-Jewish person), I have never ever been under the Law. Acts 15 is reinforced in Acts 21: 25.

d) The Jewish first day of the week goes from Saturday evening (let's say from 6.00 pm) to Sunday evening (let's say 6.00 pm). Leviticus 23:32

e) Nobody knows when Our Lord and Saviour was risen in terms of the name of the days, ie. Saturday evening or early Sunday. We do know it was <u>early on the first day of the week</u> after the Sabbath. (Remember, I am talking about Bible teachings, not what people invented outside the Bible). Let me illustrate.

Gospel, according to Mark, "Now, after He had risen early on the first day of the week, He first appeared to

Mary Magdalene, from whom He had cast out seven demons." 16:9

Now, let us narrow this down a bit.

Mark 16:1-2

"When the Sabbath was over, Mary Magdalene, and Mary the mother of James, and Salome, bought spices so that they might come and anoint Him. Very early on the first day of the week, they came to the tomb when the sun had risen."

These verses tell me that Our Lord had risen 'early on the first day of the week.' We know that Genesis Day starts in the evening, and we know the Jewish people counted the Sabbath from evening to evening. With this account, we could say that 'early on the first day of the week' could well be Saturday evening.

For argument's sake, we could also say it was after midnight that the resurrection was made on Sunday. But this argument would imply that it was around six hours onto the first day of the week, which does not fit with 'early on the first day of the week.' Also, we know that Our Lord met with Mary Magdalene 'when the sun had risen'; in terms of the day's name, it is clear it was Sunday morning.

In the Gospel of Matthew we read:

"Now after the Sabbath, as the first day of the week began to dawn, Mary Magdalene and the other Mary came to see the tomb. And behold, there was a great earthquake; for an angel of the Lord descended from heaven, and came and rolled back the stone from the door, and sat on it. His countenance was like lightning, and his clothing was as white as snow. 4 And the guards shook for fear of him and became like dead men. But the angel answered and said to the women, 'Do not be afraid, for I know that you seek Jesus who was crucified. He is not here; for He is risen, as He said. Come, see the place where the Lord lay. And go quickly and tell His disciples that He is risen from the dead, and indeed He is going before you into Galilee; there you will see Him. Behold, I have told you.' So they went out quickly from the tomb with fear and great joy, and ran to bring His disciple's word. And as they went to tell His disciples, behold, Jesus met them, saying, "Rejoice!" So they came and held Him by the feet and worshiped Him. Then Jesus said to them, "Do not be afraid. Go and tell My brethren to go to Galilee, and there they will see Me." Matthew 25: 1-9 NKJV.

This record is consistent with Mark's account. Our Lord first met with Mary Magdalene, not in the tomb but on the road and well and truly onto the day we call Sunday. But it does not say what day our Lord was resurrected.

In the Gospel, according to John, we read:

"Now, the first day of the week, Mary Magdalene went to the tomb early, while it was still dark, and saw that the stone had been taken away from the tomb. Then she ran and came to Simon Peter and to the other disciples, whom Jesus loved, and said to them, "They have taken away the Lord out of the tomb, and we do not know where they have laid Him." Peter, therefore, went out, and the other disciple, and were going to the tomb. So they both ran together, and the other disciple outran Peter and came to the tomb first. And he, stooping down and looking in, saw the linen cloths lying there, yet he did not go in. Then Simon Peter came, following him, and went into the tomb; and he saw the linen cloths lying there, and the handkerchief that had been around His head, not lying with the linen cloths, but folded together in a place by itself. Then the other disciple, who came to the tomb first, went in also, and he saw and believed. For as yet they did not know the Scripture, that He must rise again from the dead. Then, the disciples went away again to their own homes. But Mary stood outside by the tomb weeping, and as she wept, she stooped down and looked into the tomb. And she saw two angels in white sitting, one at the head and the other at the feet, where the body of Jesus had lain. Then they said to her, "Woman, why are you weeping?" She said to them,

"Because they have taken away my Lord, and I do not know where they have laid Him." Now, when she had said this, she turned around and saw Jesus standing there, and did not know that it was Jesus. Jesus said to her, "Woman, why are you weeping? Whom are you seeking?" She, supposing Him to be the gardener, said to Him, "Sir, if You have carried Him away, tell me where You have laid Him, and I will take Him away." Jesus said to her, "Mary!" She turned and said to Him, "Rabboni!" (which is to say, Teacher). Jesus said to her, "Do not cling to Me, for I have not yet ascended to My Father; but go to My brethren and say to them, 'I am ascending to My Father and your Father, and to My God and your God.' Mary Magdalene came and told the disciples that she had seen the Lord, and that He had spoken these things to her." John 20: 1-18 NKJV.

Some observations: this account is much more detailed than the other two accounts we've just seen. Still consistent with the other two, Our Lord was fully risen by Sunday morning, but it is still not clear when he actually rose (i.e., Saturday evening or Sunday morning).

Again, we know that Our Lord was up and walking around on Sunday morning, and indeed, Mary Magdalene was the first to meet Him. Notice that this account is so detailed that it describes "the handkerchief folded together by itself." It is so detailed that it tells us the Apostle John (if indeed he was the other disciple) could run faster than Peter. And yet, with all the details, it does not specify what day of the week Our Lord was resurrected. Probably because 'the first day of the week' was sufficient as far as days go. In my opinion it could also be to avoid idolatry of any certain day.

But, if we believe the Apostle's records, nobody could claim with certainty that Our Lord had risen on the day we call Sunday. We can say with all certainty that He rose on the first day of the week (Jewish first day).

The Gospel, according to Luke, reads:

"Now on the first day of the week, very early in the morning, they, and certain other women with them, came to the tomb bringing the spices which they had prepared. But they found the stone rolled away from the tomb. Then they went in and did not find the body of the Lord Jesus. And it happened, as they were greatly perplexed about this, that behold, two men stood by them in shining garments. Then, as they were afraid and bowed their faces to the earth, they said to them, "Why do you seek the living among the dead? He is not here, but is risen! Remember how He spoke to you when He was still in Galilee, saying, 'The Son of Man must be delivered into the hands of sinful men, and be crucified,

and the third day rise again.' And they remembered His words. Then they returned from the tomb and told all these things to the eleven and to all the rest. It was Mary Magdalene, Joanna, Mary the mother of James, and the other women with them, who told these things to the apostles." Luke 24: 1-10 NKJV.

Observation: Apostle Luke's record focussed on other details from the other accounts. Nonetheless, the common denominator is that it does not specify with accuracy (in terms of the name of the days) when Our Lord actually rose. In my opinion it may not be for us to know that. The Holy Spirit has given us four gospel accounts, and it decided not to disclose that aspect of the Risen Lord Jesus in any of them.

e) We know Our Lord Jesus taught the Bible on the first day of the week (On the Sunday side of it). Luke 24: 27

f) We know Our Lord Jesus met with the disciples and broke bread with them on the first day of the week (On the Sunday side of it). Luke 24: 41-43 NKJV

g) As Christians, we are directed to collect offerings on the first day of the week (Saturday evening or Sunday morning). Apostle Paul only says 'the first day of the week.' 1 Corinthians 16:2.

h) As a believing gentile, I am not commanded to observe divine congregation on the Sabbath.

i) As a believing gentile, I am not commanded to observe the divine congregation on any particular day.

j) As a Christian, I am commanded to congregate. Hebrews 10:25

Given all these points, my conscience is completely at ease if I say that I congregate on the first day of the week (The Sunday side of it).

If I find a suitable church that meets on Saturday evening, I would happily congregate there if necessary. Apparently, at some stage in the past, Christians congregated both days.

Just for completeness, I should mention that when I first started using the inductive Bible study method, I came across an interesting observation:

> *"And God <u>blessed</u> them, saying, 'Be fruitful and multiply, and fill the waters in the seas, and let birds multiply on the earth.' So the evening and the morning were the fifth day." Genesis 1: 22-23 NKJV*

> *"So God created man in His own image; in the image of God He created him; male and female He created them. Then God <u>blessed</u> them, and God said to them, 'Be*

God blessed three parts of His creation but He Blessed and Sanctified only one 'the seventh day.'

Also, notice that God created Adam and Eve on the sixth day, and among other things, they were given the job 'to fill the earth and subdue it' and the following day, God rested.

In my opinion, and bear in mind it is only my opinion, there is a very good chance that Adam and Eve rested with God on the seventh day instead of starting the job of 'subduing' the earth straight away. In that case, Adam and Eve observed the seventh day rest at least once.

Important: Theologians and biblical scholars don't like people with opinions. Only their 'scholarly opinions' count even though they don't respect the opinions of opposing denominational scholars either; otherwise, they would accept each other's opinion, which obviously they don't. Remember that they don't agree even when both camps use

217

exegesis, hermeneutics, and historical and literary interpretation mostly to rationalise their own denominational stand.

Chapter Twenty-Six – Test everything

"Do not quench the Spirit. Do not despise prophecies. Test all things; hold fast to what is good. Abstain from every form of evil." 1 Thessalonians 5: 19-22

I remember the first time I studied this passage I thought it meant in terms of doctrinal views of men in the end times. Then, one night during a Bible study group meeting, we came across the following passage:

"Not everyone who says to Me, 'Lord, Lord,' shall enter the kingdom of heaven, but he who does the will of My Father in heaven. Many will say to Me on that day, 'Lord, Lord, have we not prophesied in Your name, cast out demons in Your name, and done many wonders in Your name?' And then I will declare to them, 'I never knew you; depart from Me, you who practice lawlessness!' Matthew 7: 21-23 NKJV

We were participating and sharing our thoughts mostly along the lines of: 'false prophets using emotions and manipulating people,' 'false healings and miracles,' 'false prophets doing signs and wonders,' 'false prophets that get rich with false miracles,' and similar ideas. But one sister made a very particular observation. She said 'notice that it says "who says to me" and "will say to." We all agreed with that observation, but I don't think we realise the significance of it at the time.

That night, driving on my way home, I was meditating on that passage, and I remembered a passage when Our Lord told the disciples not to stop people from using His name to perform miracles.

When I got home, I looked for the verse, but I did not remember it correctly; it had to do with casting out demons.

> *"Now John answered Him, saying, "Teacher, we saw someone who does not follow us casting out demons in Your name, and we forbade him because he does not follow us." But Jesus said, "Do not forbid him, for no one who works a miracle in My name can soon afterward speak evil of Me. For he who is not against us is on our side." Mark 9: 38-40 NKJV*

I noticed the universality of the Words of Our Lord, and I also noticed that in this case, it is Apostle John who testifies of that person casting out demons in Jesus' name.

This passage seems to contradict our passage in Matthew 7, but it does not. The passage in Matthew 7 warns us against false prophets and how to identify them by their fruits, which include their own claims of performing miracles. Remember "who says to me" and "will say to me." In Mark's passage, it is Apostle John who makes the claim that somebody else is performing miracles in the Lord's name. The miracle has been witnessed and testified by another person other than the one performing the miracle. This is very significant. I reviewed most of the miracles performed by our Lord and the disciples, and I noticed very important characteristics:

1- There were people who knew and testified of the original condition of the receiver of the miracle.

2- The persons receiving the miracle testified themselves about it.

3- The miracle happened, and eyewitnesses verified the facts surrounding the miracles. Sometimes, the miracles had to be verified by asking relatives of the afflicted person, friends, or sometimes town folks who saw the person just hanging around public places in their previous condition and just volunteered the information confirming the before and after. Always, somebody who knew the recipient of the healing confirmed that a miracle had taken place.

4- Most distinguishable: Miracles were reported in the Scriptures by another disciple or witness, never by the one performing the miracles. (Even in Luke 10:17, nobody claims a miracle personally, only a general report of their mission:

This is where "test all things; hold fast what is good" becomes so relevant.

These 'claimers' of Matthew 7: 21-23 are so common that those claims are becoming suburban folklore. The details may vary a bit, but in general, the modus operandi is basically the same, and you hear similar accounts all around.

Example 1

Have you ever heard of the Pastor or Evangelist who said he/she heard God calling him/her to step down from a bus while travelling home at the end of the day and was directed to preach under a bridge or a back ally where there were drug addicts and derelicts and as result of his/her preaching some of them started crying and repenting and accepting Jesus as their Saviour. At the end of the story the said preacher would shout praises to the Lord. It looks like they are praising the Lord, but the reality is that they are praising themselves.

Example 2

Have you heard of the preacher who received a message from God to call or visit a person of the congregation, and that phone call or visit stopped the person from committing suicide? Again, after they tell that story in their churches, they start shouting praises to the Lord when it is very clear they are praising themselves as 'humble vessels' of the Lord.

Example 3

Have you heard of the preacher who claims he/she prayed for a person with a mangled extremity, and it regenerated in front of him or grew longer or something along those lines, and immediately after telling the story, he/she starts shouting praises to the Lord? In reality, they are praising themselves 'as conduits' of God's healing. Sometimes, they don't even try to disguise it. They just say, 'Thank you, God, for using me when I don't deserve to be used' or something like that.

Example 4

Have you heard of the preacher who comes out to the stage in front of the congregation and starts shouting, 'I remember when the deaf person received the gift of hearing in that corner, I remember when the paraplegic person started walking on that side of the church, and the blind person received the gift of sight right here in front of me, then he/she starts shouting praises to the Lord, but they are really praising themselves.

Example 5

Have you heard about the pastor who was confronted in a dark alley by some criminals, and suddenly, they ran away? Later, the pastor finds out it was because there were angels behind him protecting him. After telling something like this again, the preacher would normally shout praises to the Lord, 'Thank you for using me and protecting me, your humble servant' etc., etc. It looks like they are praising God, but they are flattering themselves.

Example 6

Have you heard of the pro-gun preacher who was arguing with a pacifist, and God shows the pro-gun preacher that the pacifist has guns in his house?

Again, I have to say the details may change according to audiences and cultures, but all these types of accounts have one thing in common. They are related by the preachers, not by witnesses, and most importantly, never verified. We don't have to take any self-proclaimed accounts by 'faith.'

We have to test everything as our duty as believers of the Word of God.

Compare all these examples with Matthew 7: 21-23, 'they say this they say that' and Our Lord does not like at all.

Consider the following account:

> "You are sitting at a service on a Sunday morning at your church. Somebody comes in the middle of proceedings, walking up the centre aisle with two people accompanying him. These people have the dirty appearance, dishevelled, and badly presented. One of them walks up to the front of the congregation, turns around, and declares, 'The other night I was under a bridge, your preacher came and preached to us. I felt the words touching my heart, and I cried and repented of my sins, and now I want to follow Jesus; these are my friend, who saw this, and they want to know more also."

I made this up to make a clear contrast with the previous examples.

In this case, as in the Bible cases, the person receiving the blessing is witnessing; he brought along two witnesses, the preacher in question kept his part humbly in his heart, and the whole congregation participated in the process.

So different from just the preacher giving himself/herself all the glory disguised as giving glory to God.

> *"But when you do a charitable deed, do not let your left hand know what your right hand is doing." Matthew 6:3 NKJV*

Note: I already mentioned that I believe in the 'signs that will follow believers' as this is an actual conditional universal promise made by Our Lord as recorded by the Holy Spirit in the Gospel of Mark 16: 17-18.

In regards to divine healing, I can confidently say that God does heal and does not heal. Apostle Paul had to leave behind some companions because they got sick (2 Timothy 4:20). In my personal experience, I can testify that at least once, I got better after a person prayed for me. On other occasions, nothing happened.

Application: If I consider all the characteristics surrounding Biblical miracles, then I am entitled to ask for proof that a miracle took place. I should not trust miracle claims just for the sake of it. The commandment is 'to test all things,' often to unmask false prophets in the end times. Asking for proof of claimed miracles demonstrates my faith and trust in the Word of God.

Chapter Twenty-Seven - Do not deviate

"The Lord will give them over to you, that you may do to them according to every commandment which I have commanded you. <u>Be strong and of good courage</u>, do not fear nor be afraid of them; for the Lord your God, He is the One who goes with you. He will not leave you nor forsake you." Then Moses called Joshua and said to him in the sight of all Israel, "<u>Be strong and of good courage,</u> for you must go with this people to the land which the Lord has sworn to their fathers to give them, and you shall cause them to inherit it. 8 And the Lord, He is the One who goes before you. He will be with you; He will not leave you nor forsake you; do not fear nor be dismayed." Deuteronomy 31: 5-8 NKJV

Observation: The Lord will give their enemies over to them. I thought, why was the exhortation to be strong and courageous when the battle was won already?

Then, in verse 23:

"Then He inaugurated Joshua, the son of Nun, and said, "Be strong and of good courage; for you shall bring the children of Israel into the land of which I swore to them, and I will be with you."

Again, Moses calls Joshua "to be strong and of good courage." Don't get me wrong, even with God on our side; our human nature may easily succumb in front of a historic event in front of us.

And now God shows us where our strength and courage should be focussed:

> *"No man shall be able to stand before you all the days of your life; as I was with Moses, so I will be with you. I will not leave you nor forsake you. Be strong and of good courage, for to this people you shall divide as an inheritance the land which I swore to their fathers to give them. Only be strong and very courageous, that you may observe to do according to all the law which Moses, My servant, commanded you; do not turn from it to the right hand or to the left, that you may prosper wherever you go. This Book of the Law shall not depart from your mouth, but you shall meditate in it day and night, that you may observe to do according to all that is written in it. For then you will make your way prosperous, and then you will have good success. Have I not commanded you? Be strong and of good courage; do not be afraid, nor be dismayed, for the Lord your God is with you wherever you go." Joshua 1: 5-9 NKJV*

I find this passage so edifying. Never did God instruct His people in military strategies or hand-to-hand combat. He gave them victory. But when it comes to obeying His Word, it is up to the individual, and the same advice to 'be strong and of good courage' applies to confronting giant enemies as it applies to our personal commitment not to deviate from His Word.

I thought for a while that applying a proper system of studying the Bible would result in a unified view of the doctrines given there to us. But I proved to be wrong. There are exegetical rules, hermeneutical rules, and historical and literary interpretation rules, but in the end, there are myriads of conflicting doctrines of men studied and created using those theological methods out there waiting to confuse me.

But I have to be strong and courageous myself to adhere to the Word of God and only to the Word of God. These doctrines of men will lay to my left and to my right, but I should walk straight by just following the Word of God.

Is it easy? Not at all. Every time I claim I don't believe in this or that doctrine invented by men, I get looks as if I was some sort of creature from outer space. Denominational churches are known to adopt this or that doctrine of men, or this or that creed or confession of faith determined in some council somewhere in time. Is it harmful to believe these doctrines of men? I don't know, but I strongly suspect that because they contradict themselves, something is seriously wrong. I know for sure that only the Word of God shows us the correct way to walk in faith. The Bible warns us that, as humans, we are not to trust our own understanding:

Application: I borrow the following for my personal application.

> *"Trust in the Lord with all your heart, and lean not on your own understanding; in all your ways acknowledge Him, and He shall direct your paths." Proverbs 3:5-6 NKJV*

Chapter Twenty-Eight – Science vs religion

In a world where, even in Christian circles, Genesis's account of creation is referred to as a 'myth' in order to conform to the world, I felt it necessary to talk a little about the topic of science from my point of view. I will not sell out my belief in God's creation.

"But you, Daniel, shut up the words and seal the book until the time of the end; many shall run to and fro, and knowledge shall increase." Daniel 12:4 NKJV

Observation: It is interesting that the verse links the increase of knowledge to the end days. As if knowledge is always there, but in the last days, the increase in knowledge will be noticeable or significant.

I read commentaries about this verse in relation to 'knowledge,' and the experts relate 'knowledge' to knowing God, which would be in contrast to:

"For false Christs and false prophets will rise and show great signs and wonders to deceive, if possible, even the elect." Matthew 24:24 NKJV.

Let me say it from the start. I don't have a quarrel with science, but let me make this very clear: 'evolution' is not science.

There are several philosophical approaches to describe science. People like Thomas Kuhn and Karl Popper made great contributions to the concepts of the elements of scientific definitions, and of course, there is a substantial body of literature that has expanded from those initial attempts. The literature delves into concepts such as relativism, positivism, neo-positivism, irrationality, and empiricism; you name it, and whatever you want to name, there is a good chance that there is there somewhere. It is not my purpose to deal with any of these.

The easiest way for me to talk about science consists of two premises:

The first premise is that I call it 'Science and Technology' instead of just science. This is a practical way to acknowledge the positive influence of the scientific mind in our lives.

For example, I am writing this on a laptop (science and technology), and I am wearing glasses to see better (science and technology). Science and technology can actually land a probe on another planet and get relevant information about that planet. I can talk and see my relatives on the other side of the globe with my mobile phone (science and technology). The advancements in science and technology in the area of medicine are astonishing. Knowledge is indeed increasing.

The second premise is to understand the basic concepts of the scientific method.

1- Observation of phenomena.

2- Thesis or a causal theory of the phenomena (if this and this, then that).

3- Hypotheses.

4- Testing. (replicable)

5- Analysing data.

6- Accept or reject hypotheses.

7 – Synthesis. (Conclusions and predictions within the variables used)

The scientific experimental method is a proven system to increase and use knowledge.

This is where we come to a crossroads. If it cannot be tested, is it in the realm of science or philosophy?

I know that when it comes to God, it is a matter of belief and faith.

I know that when it comes to real proper science, it is a matter of experimental testing.

When it comes to the theory of evolution, who knows?

(For a most scholarly definition of the scientific work, visit: Definitions of Fact, Theory, and Law in Scientific Work | National Center for Science Education (ncse.ngo) as of 26-03-2024)[5]

This is where things get fussy. People think that evolution is scientific, but it is not. It looks scientific, and scientific tools can be used in investigating it, but in the end, the theory cannot be tested. The most it can be claimed is that 'evidence points out to this or that.'

An easy way to see this is by saying 'evolution and technology' and making a list of technological achievements derived from the theory of evolution. And yes, I will call it a theory until there is an experimental test to prove the contrary. In my opinion, experimental testing is the basis of

---

[5] Definitions of Fact, Theory, and Law in Scientific Work | National Center for Science Education (ncse.ngo)

scientific advancement. Huxley claimed evolution is a fact but could not prove it, and that is a fact.

Another simple test to demonstrate evolution is not scientific. In the last two hundred years, real science has made enormous advances in all fronts of the hard sciences. These advances were obtained by the correct use of the scientific method. It is a process of refinement, to be sure, but it is a proven method.

Compare that with evolution theory. Two hundred years ago, they claimed 'we come from the monkeys; today, they show their scientific advancement by claiming 'we come from ape-like creatures.'

The most it can be demonstrated is adaptation. And this is where the evolutionists' god 'time' comes to play an important part in their theory. 'Time' became their pet god. A good example of their god 'time' can be seen in statements similar to: 'DNA gained information in nature millions of years ago, and we don't see that happening anymore in nature, but it will happen again millions of years in the future.' I have read articles describing how some water-living organisms adapt to the changes in the chemical composition of their environment, and the adaptation is called 'evolutionary change' or the organism 'evolved' or similar terminology. Keep in mind that the organism is still the same organism. It did not evolve into a different species of organism. My guess is that if they don't use the word 'evolution,' those articles would not be published. If they only talk of adaptation, those articles would never see the light of day.

This is what they teach new scientists:

"Evolution as fact and not theory." Examples:

'Other commentators – focusing on the changes in species over generations, and in some cases, common ancestry – have stressed, in order to emphasize the weight of supporting evidence, that evolution is a fact, arguing that the use of the term "theory" is not useful:

Richard Lewontin wrote, "It is time for students of the evolutionary process, especially those who have been misquoted and used by the creationists, to state clearly that evolution is fact, not theory."[36]

Douglas J. Futuyma writes in Evolutionary Biology (1998), "The statement that organisms have descended with modifications from common ancestors – the historical reality of evolution – is not a theory. It is a fact, as fully as the fact of the earth's revolution about the sun."[6]

Richard Dawkins says, "One thing all real scientists agree upon is the fact of evolution itself. It is a fact that we are cousins of gorillas, kangaroos, starfish, and bacteria. Evolution is as much a fact as the heat of the sun. It is not a theory, and for pity's sake, let's stop confusing the philosophically naive by calling it so. Evolution is a fact."[37]

Neil Campbell wrote in his 1990 biology textbook, "Today, nearly all biologists acknowledge that evolution is a fact. The term theory is no longer appropriate except when referring to the various models that attempt to explain how life evolves ... it is important to understand that the current questions about how life evolves in no way imply any disagreement over the fact of evolution."[38]

https://en.wikipedia.org/wiki/Evolution_as_fact_and_theory#:~:text=Miller%20writes%2C%20%22evolution%20is%20as%20much,as%20anything%20we%20know%20in%20science.%22&text=Miller%20writes%2C%20%22evolution%20is,we%20know%20in%20science.%22&text=%22ev

<u>olution%20is%20as%20much,as%20anything%20we%20k
now</u> as at 27-03-2024.[6]

They are brainwashing young scientists to claim evolution is a fact because they cannot actually prove it.

They should be ashamed of themselves. Work harder and prove it; do not lie to people. Follow the example of real scientists in the real sciences. It is funny how they talked about 'how life evolved,' and they don't even know what life is. They can see the mechanics of live organisms but that is about all. If you want to have a good laugh, check out one scientific definition of life:

"All groups of living organisms share several key characteristics or functions: order, sensitivity or response to stimuli, reproduction, adaptation, growth and development, regulation, homeostasis, and energy processing. When viewed together, these characteristics serve to define life."

---

[6]

<u>https://en.wikipedia.org/wiki/Evolution_as_fact_and_theory#:~:text=M
iller%20writes%2C%20%22evolution%20is%20as%20much,as%20an
ything%20we%20know%20in%20science.%22&text=Miller%20writes
%2C%20%22evolution%20is,we%20know%20in%20science.%22&te
xt=%22evolution%20is%20as%20much,as%20anything%20we%20kn
ow</u>

https://pressbooks.umn.edu/introbio/chapter/definition-of-life/ as at 27/03/2024.[7]

Of course, this defines nothing. This is what is normally referred to as 'circular reasoning.'

Look at my 'scientific' definition of life:

"Life is what makes organisms live." LOL

I remember that, in primary school, they used to teach evolution by mentioning the British moth. During the Industrial Revolution, as part of a suburban beautification program, the city councils painted tree trunks white. The prevalent moths at the time were darkish in colour, and of course when they sat on the tree trunk to rest, they were easy targets for the birds, so they adapted to the environment by camouflaging their appearance with a lighter colour. When the cities could not afford the beautification process anymore and stopped painting the tree trunks white, and again the poor moths became easy targets, so they reverted back to a darker colour. I remember clearly they taught me that as an example of evolution. Of course, it is not. If it was evolution when the moths turned lighter, then it would be de-evolution

---

[7] https://pressbooks.umn.edu/introbio/chapter/definition-of-life/

when they turned back to their initial darkish colour. Please give me a break.

This is a clear example of adaptation, and this is when evolutionists run to the altar of their god "time." The claim is that if the change is 'evolutionary,' then within millions of years in the future, the moths will turn into a new species. (A crude description, but basically, it covers their premise). Are we supposed to accept that type of speculation?

Adaptive capabilities in species do not prove evolution.

I don't have any problems believing that our human bodies share certain biological characteristics with some animals on earth; call them cousins, if you like. We are part of the same creation process on the same earth. It makes sense that God knew about gravitational forces, alkalinity, salinity, electric and magnetic forces, chemical composition, radiation, solar flares, and other physical realities of planet Earth, and given that we are all living under the same common physical earthly conditions, it should not be surprising that God gave us some common bodily characteristics necessary to survive on earth.

I strongly believe that God gave His creation the ability to adapt, and I have no problem with the concept of adaptation. I have serious problems with the idea of mixing adaptation with the god of evolutionists, 'time,' and concluding that combination will produce 'evolution' and, what is even worse, present it as 'scientific.'

I can also say that God created the strong force, the weak force, dynamic energy, kinetic energy, electromagnetism, the wave function, and absolutely everything else. Piece of cake for God.

I could also make the bold statement that 'the microbiological meme' is still in the miracle basket. LOL

Now, to find the 'graviton,' my guess is that a much larger particle accelerator might be needed (the circumference of the Equator came to mind) or a miracle. I am sitting on the fence with this one.

The problem is that the theory of evolution hides behind the hard sciences. Hard experimental science earned the right to be respected by the results obtained by practicing and refining rigorous scientific experimental methods of investigation over the years. Just by looking again at the examples on 'evolution is a fact' I quoted above, you will see how they are 'free-riding' on the achievements of others:

Douglas J. Futuyma claimed that evolution is a fact: "It is a fact, as fully as the fact of the earth's revolution about the sun," <u>free-riding</u> on an actual fact that has nothing to do with the theory of evolution.

Richard Lewontin wrote, "It is time for students of the evolutionary process, especially those who have been misquoted and used by the creationists, to state clearly that evolution is fact, not theory." Really sir? Shouldn't you motivate the students of the evolutionary process to perfect their experimental design skills in order to prove evolution, not to just 'state it' as a fact when it is obvious by your own statement it is not?

Richard Dawkins says, "One thing all real scientists agree upon is the fact of evolution itself. It is a fact that we are cousins of gorillas, kangaroos, starfish, and bacteria. Evolution is as much a fact as the heat of the sun. It is not a theory, and for pity's sake, let's stop confusing the philosophically naive by calling it so. Evolution is a fact."

Notice how this statement 'free ride' on "all real scientists" and "as much a fact as the heat of the sun." It is so blunt the linear association 'real scientists agree' then immediately 'fact that we are cousins' (which, by the way, doesn't prove anything) then 'evolution is as much a fact as the heat of the sun (theory of evolution trying to get respect by association) and finally 'stop confusion by calling it' evolution is a fact.

Notice 'calling' it, not 'proving' it. The statement tries to establish a link between real scientists and the theory of evolution and wraps it up by 'calling it.'

Neil Campbell wrote in his 1990 biology textbook, "Today, nearly all biologists acknowledge that evolution is a fact." The statement is <u>free-riding</u> on 'biologists.' By the way, no biologist or other experimental scientist will claim anything outside the realm of their experimental design and the variables and constraints used in those. Campbell goes on, "The term theory is no longer appropriate except when referring to the various models that attempt to explain how life evolves." What? Is the term theory only valid when you are trying to explain evolution? What?

I don't want to appear disrespectful to any of these distinguished people. They are all experts in their field and respected authors. I like to pay my respects, especially to those who passed away.

The fact remains that the theory of evolution is still nothing more than a theory. Apart from some people agreeing it is not. Agreement of opinions does not make it a fact.

I was perusing The Greatest Show on Earth by Richard Dawkins and came across this statement regarding his previous books in the preface:

"Looking back on those books, I realised that the evidence for evolution itself was nowhere explicitly set out and that this was a serious gap I needed to close."

I bought the book, and I read it from cover to cover. It is a fascinating book, and I recommend it. But again, it does not prove evolution. Just by looking at the description of the Lenski experiment, comment on things like 'what this evolutionary change suggests' when there is no evolutionary change. There is adaptability change. I don't like it when they use the word 'evolution' to the point that it becomes a disguised use of 'circular reasoning.'

I read "The Evolution Of A Key Innovation In An Experimental Population Of Escherichia Coli: A Tale Of Opportunity, Contingency, And Co-option" by Zachary David Blount. This is, of course, a scientific paper using experimentation as a method of investigation, and my congratulations go to all experimental evolutionists. They are trying their hearts out, and I think if I wanted to prove evolution, I would go about it by experimentation.

However, I am still very touchy about the use of 'evolved,' 'evolutionary,' 'evolution,' and similar terminology, especially when describing adaptability changes. For instance, "The evolution of the Cit+ trait involved three successive processes: potentiation, actualization, and refinement." Why the use of the word 'evolution?' Nothing evolved. Words like appeared, developed, manifested, or adapted, I think, are a lot more accurate.

I find the word 'evolution' and its derivatives thrown around in 'scientific magazines' so often for any type of adaptation that it seems as if the authors are trying to convince themselves of evolution. The 'evolution' word is thrown around like confetti at a parade. Just because you use the word evolution a lot, it does not prove anything. I sympathize with the evolutionist's predicament. They start with the hypothesis that there is evolution and then try to prove it instead of trying to disprove it. I know it is a hard position. The null hypotheses should be: there is no evolution and then take it from there. But no, they start with a double false null hypotheses: there is evolution.

But let us get back to the paper. First of all, let me apologise at the outset for my lack of microbiologist knowledge among the lack of other knowledge as well. Also, let me clarify that my following comment is in no way critical of this paper as this paper passed the scrutiny of its peers, so it is absolutely valid and scientific. Not that it needs my validation, either.

I have one little question in regard to this statement, though:

"However, the inability to use citrate as a carbon source under oxic conditions is a species-defining trait of E. coli."

My question is:

What if E.coli always had in it the ability to use citrate as a carbon source under oxic conditions, but it never needed to use this ability, and therefore, it was never detected? This would mean that this defining trait of the species was wrongly diagnosed.

If that is the case, all that can be claimed is that after short of 31500 cloned generations, that ability was found to manifest in a weak format, and then the trait was passed on to other generations increasingly stronger. Then I don't think it can be claimed that the ability 'evolved' as it was dormant on the E.coli all the time.

The idea of the paper was that 'historical contingency' was debated as a factor in 'evolution,' but it had never before been empirically demonstrated, and the paper sought to settle the debate by experimentation.

Again, I don't know enough, and I am too old, too poor, and too disinterested to pursue this, but I still say that 'the theory of evolution' is still a theory. I accept that outside stimulation applied methodically and gradually will tend to generate a reaction from the target organism, whether it will adapt to survive the external stimulus or not. But I don't accept that this proves 'evolution.' I never checked all the relevant material mentioned in the paper regarding experimental design, so I don't know how many experiments were conducted to arrive at the correct doses of the various stimulants used on the sample populations. By the way, the distinct populations resulting from experimentation were still mutant E.coli populations, but E.coli nonetheless.

Let me reiterate: I have a lot of respect for the scientific community. I don't have a problem with the scientific method, but I do question the motives of Dr. Dawkins, for instance, who, even in his very good monogram, makes statements like 'the creationists hate it.' Why resent those who kept their faith? You abandoned your faith. No worries. Just keep on moving and let those who kept their faith alone. (I really should not say it is ok to abandon your faith; I like to encourage you to return to your faith in God, as naïve as this sounds, I have to say it)

Anyway, I have to disagree with Dr. Dawkins, and again, I have to apologise for my ignorance, but cloning something 31500 times with antibiotics and other chemicals employed in the process hardly qualifies as 'new information entering genomes without the intervention of a designer.' In my ignorance, I call this particular intelligent designer Dr. Blount.

Also, Dr. Dawkins's creationists argued that new information entering genomes is not observable in nature. As far as I know, they never claimed that it could not be manipulated under laboratory conditions.

However, I think that focusing on the mechanics of change is missing the bigger picture. Regardless of how sophisticated the experiments are, all they can observe are the mechanics of change under specific induced circumstances.

When I first read 'On the Origin of the Species,' I was very young, but I still remember the first question that popped into my head. Why would species want to survive? Years later, when I went to high school, I asked my biology teacher, and she didn't tell me anything new when she answered 'survival instinct.'

'Survival instinct' is a total cop-out, which explains nothing. Today, my question would be, 'Why is the gene selfish?' 'How does the gene know that it wants to keep on living?' How does the amygdala know what a threat is, and how does it know it has to avoid it in order to keep on living? What micro neuro-physiological process (thought or consciousness if you like) has to happen for the amygdala or the reptilian brain or whatever is in there to realise that it is alive and wants to keep on living?

Let me put it more plainly. Why would organisms go to the trouble of finding suitable environments to be born, grow, reproduce, and die? What is in it for them? Please don't say 'survival instinct' or 'survival of the species'; that inane reply is lazy, pathetic, and useless, and it hasn't explained anything new in the last two hundred years.

But enough of this.

There was indeed an infamous dispute between Galileo and the Roman Catholic Church. This dispute had nothing to do with God, the Bible, or science. There is nothing in the Bible in relation to the centre of the planetary system or the centre of the universe, for that matter.

Application: The verse in the book of Daniel prophetically tells me that in the end times, 'knowledge will increase.' My job is to discern proper real knowledge achieved by experimental science from speculative evidential pseudo-scientific knowledge. This is a big job. So, instead, I will be happy enough to use the 'science and technology' aspect of knowledge, which is indeed increasing.

Epilogue

I am pleased to say the 'el chico Roberto' became Pastor Roberto San Martin. He and his family became a pillar of the evangelical movement for the Spanish speaking community in Brisbane.

The young gnostic South American couple that gave me the gnostic book received Jesus as their Lord and Saviour, and after fifty years, they are still committed Baptist believers.

Me? I have regrets to fill out many pages in my notebooks but I am happy to say that I have returned to my first love, the Bible. Simple and plain no doctrines of men at all as in the beginning.

I am also pleased to see that regardless of theological differences, there are millions of Christian believers doing the groundwork with their own feet to spread the gospel. Glory to God.

Wow! What a journey, and it is not finished yet. There are different ways to find our own corner of spiritual sanity. I found it in the devotional act of studying the Bible using the inductive Bible study method as my corner of spiritual sanity. I call this study 'within' in contrast to 'without or external to the Word.' I tried hard to reconcile Christian doctrines invented by man with their counterparts' Christian doctrines, which were also invented by man, and I just did not make any progress at all. I decided that for me, the only way was to not believe in any of them. They contradict each other. How much worse could I do? I am not as dogmatic and inflexible as to think that other people cannot read the same passages that I read and get a more correct insight than I do. I am sure that this is the case anyway.

I understand that we all need clear guidance and guidelines in order to have a clear starting point, and in that regard, I can appreciate the efforts these theologians make to, at least at a denominational level, present clear perspectives from their point of view. I just wanted to share my experiences, up and downs, ideas, struggles, and my journey to find my spiritual 'sanity', and I make no apologies for this. All of my 'findings' are rough and not very elegant, but I spent a lot of quality hours of fellowship with the Word in this endeavour, and it proved to be very edifying and liberating for me. I hope that my journey may be of inspiration to you. If you are struggling with the various doctrines of men out there and you are confused and disoriented, the Bible in its purest form may be the answer for you as it was for me.

I often meditate about my journey driving my white car (I nicknamed it 'el blanquito') through the streets of Ipswich on Sunday mornings going to church. I enjoy the empty streets of Ipswich Road, clear of congestion going at the speed limit, feeling the warm welcoming of a sunny day in front of me it seems surreal. And when I come out from the church, and make my way to the car park, a warm feeling invades me, there waiting for me uncompromisingly faithful 'el blanquito.'

God Bless.

Bibliography

Biblia de Estudio de la Vida Plena Reina-Valera 1960, Editorial Vida, Miami, 1993.

Cornish, Rick, 5 Minute Theologian: Maximum Truth in Minimum Time, NavPress, Colorado Springs, 2004.

Dawkins, Richard, The God Delusion, Bantam Press, London, 2006.

Dawkins, Richard, The Greatest Show on Earth, Black Swan edition, Transworld Publishers, London, 2010.

Douglas J.D. and Tenney Merrill C., Zondervan Bible Dictionary, NIV version, Zondervan, Grand Rapids, 2008.

Erickson, Millard J., Christian Theology, third edition, Baker Academic, Grand Rapids, 2013.

Goodrick, Edward W. and Kohlenberger III, John R, The Strongest NIV Exhaustive Concordance, Zondervan, Michigan, 1999.

Gorman, Michael J., Elements of Biblical Exegesis, Revised and Expanded Edition: A Basic Guide for Students and Ministers, Baker Academic, Grand Rapids, 2009.

Green, Jay P. Sr., The Interlinear Bible including the Hebrew-Aramaic Old Testament and the Greek-English New Testament, Hendrickson Publishers, Peabody, 1985.

Hendricks, Howard G. and Hendricks William D., Living by the Book: The Art and Science of Reading the Bible, Moody Publishers, Chicago, 2007.

Hiitchens, Christopher, God is not Great: How religion poisons everything, Allen & Unwin, Crows Nest, 2008.

Kent, Keri Wyatt, Deeper into the Word New Testament: Reflections on 100 Words from the New Testament, Bethany House, Minneapolis, 2011.

Kent, Keri Wyatt, Deeper into the Word Old Testament: Reflections on 100 Words from the Old Testament, Bethany House, Minneapolis, 2011.

Kohlenberger III, John R., Zondervan NIV Nave's Topical Bible, Zondervan Publishing, Grand Rapids, 1994.

Litfin, Bryan M., Getting to Know the Church Fathers: An Evangelical Introduction, Baker Academic, Grand Rapids, 2016.

Marshall, H. I., Millard, A. R., Packer J. I. and Wiseman, D. J., New Bible Dictionary, third edition, Intervarsity Press, Leicester, 1996.

Marx, Karl and Engels, Frederick, On Religion, Progress Publishers, Moscow, 1975.

Milne, Bruce, Know the Truth: A Handbook of Christian Belief, Third Edition, Inter-Varsity Press, Nottingham, 2009.

NIV Study Bible, Zondervan, Michigan, 2008 update.

Robertson, Archibald, Socialism and Religion: an Essay, Lawrence & Wishart, London, 1960.

Serendipity Bible: For Personal and Small Group Study, New International Version, Zondervan, Grand Rapids, 1998.

Shermer, Michael, How We Believe: Science, Scepticism, and the Search for God, Second Edition, Henry Holt and Company, New York, 2000.

Strauss, Mark L., How to Read the Bible in Changing Times: Understanding and Applying the Word of God Today, Baker Books, Grand Rapids, 2011.

Tenney, Merrill C., Pictorial Encyclopedia of the Bible in Five Volumes, Zondervan, Grand Rapids, 1976.

The King James Study Bible, Thomas Nelson, Nashville, 1981.

The NKJV Study Bible 2nd Edition, Thomas Nelson, Nashville, 2007.

Vanhoozer, Kevin J., Dictionary for Theological Interpretation of the Bible, Baker Academic, Grand Rapids, 2005.

Warren, Rick, Rick Warren's Bible Study Methods: Twelve Ways you can Unlock God's Word, Zondervan, Grand Rapids, 2006.

Young, Lloyd, Young's Analytical Concordance to the Bible, King James version, Thomas Nelson, Nashville, 1982.

Young, Robert, Young's Literal Translation of the Holy Bible, Revised Edition, Baker Book House, Grand Rapids.

Zondervan Handbook to the Bible, Zondervan, Grand Rapids, 1999.

Appendix A - Basic Inductive Bible Study Template.

Adapted from various sources by Ed Cubilla

Baselines: God knows the end from the beginning- pray for wisdom, understanding and the guidance of the Holy Spirit- The Word of God is eternal and in effect today- allow for literary forms, and I will look at the context around it: Verse, chapter, book, the whole counsel of the Bible- If the passage is not clear then I follow with: scriptures interpret scriptures'- scriptures interpret the scriptures'-Apply principle of first appearance-if the verse still unclear: Keep it in your heart and wait until it develops more clearly for you-final step: Ask, consult, read books, watch instructional videos and investigate commentaries (but be cautious as answers could have doctrinal bias).

Verse	Step 1 Observation	Step 2 Interpretation/Insights	Step 3 Application
Write or quote the verse or passage here.	**Investigate the passage, ask questions, and notice statements in the verse.** WHO is speaking? WHAT is this about? Who are the main characters? TO WHOM is the author speaking? What is the subject or event covered in the chapter? What do you learn about the people, event, or teaching? WHEN do/will the events occur or did/will something happen to someone in particular? (Keep an eye for words such as: now, until, then, when and after) WHERE did or will this happen? Where was it said? WHY is something being said or mentioned? Why would/will this happen? Why at that time and/or to this person/people?	**Paraphrase the verse: or summarise the verse or passage in your own words** **Identify the type of writing**: Is it describing an event (Characters, place, time, story, plot: something happens, character reacts)? Is it a parable? An illustration? Poetic? Is it a lecture/discourse? (a clear lesson, a teaching? **Answer the questions generated from your observations.** Use your Study Bible or other reference material available to you. **Find insights :** - Look for a single meaning in the passage; let the passage speak by itself. - Start by taking the passage at its literal value; what the Bible says is what the Bible says, and it is what the Bible means. Context within the Bible: Verse, paragraph, chapter, book, the whole counsel of the Bible.	**Relate to your experience** Having made the observations, answered questions and summarised the significant insights for us, we can now ask: Have I ever been in a similar situation? How can I follow the lesson or example in the passage? Is it important to follow the insights I gained? Is there anything resembling the situation in the passage that is closest to me? **Write a statement to summarise your application.**
Make dot points of statements that are significant and self-explanatory.	**Summarising interpretations/insights** Write notes on anything you discovered that is significant to you.	**Plan of action** What can I do to take action on my application in the near future?

www.ingramcontent.com/pod-product-compliance
Lightning Source LLC
Chambersburg PA
CBHW040859010826
48978CB00013BA/1087